mia's
HearT

a paradise diaries novel

by Courtney Cole

Lakehouse Press, 2012

This book is an original publication of Lakehouse Press.
All rights reserved.

Cover photography and design by Dani Snell, Refracting Light Photography
Cover Models: Tyler Martin and Vanessa Sifuentes

Library of Congress Cataloging-in-Publication Data

Cole, Courtney.
        Mia's Heart/Courtney Cole --- Lakehouse Press trade pbk.ed.
        ISBN: 978-0615735177

Printed in the United States of America

Dedication

To My Daughter.
My littlest writing assistant and
Biggest fan.
I will love you forever and ever and ever.

courtney cole

"Paradise was made for tender hearts;
Hell, for loveless hearts."
- Voltaire

Chapter One

Five times.

That's how many times I have looked at the clock while my mother has been lecturing me.

Five hundred times.

That's how many times I've wished I could ram a sharp stick into my ears to prevent myself from having to listen. The ruptured ear drum would be So. Worth. It.

But unfortunately, I'll need my hearing for my senior year this year. And also unfortunately, I can tell by the bright red hue to my mother's cheeks that she's far from finished.

I sigh and stare out the window.

And ponder my life.

Because I live in a bubble.

A fragile, beautiful, misleading bubble.

Anyone looking in might think that life within my shiny bubble is perfect. That I have the perfect parents, perfect home, a perfect life. But it is far from perfect and so am I.

Trust me.

Or just ask my mother.

"Take it out."

Each word that Adrianna Giannis spits from her lips is like an ice pellet. She's really pissed now, I can tell. But I don't care because I'm pissed, too. My new nose ring isn't hurting anyone. It's just a little silver stud. It's not like I got a tattoo on my face or my nipples pierced. I tell her that and her nostrils flare out a little and she cocks her head in a very dangerous way.

I take a cautionary step back. My mother has never laid a hand on me, but all good things must come to an end sometime.

That time might seriously be now.

Mom narrows her eyes and I might be mistaken, but I think I see red in them.

"Mia Alexandria Giannis. We have put up with your black clothing and the way you dye your hair. We have even tolerated your new bad attitude. But this." And at this point, she throws up her hands and waves them around. "This is ridiculous. You *know* that we have an image to protect because of your father. You know that. Yet you don't seem to care. You don't care about anything but yourself. What are we going to do with you?"

I stare back at her as firmly as I can and take a deep breath.

And then reluctantly dive back into the same-old, same-old argument that we've already had five hundred other times before.

Make that five-thousand.

Or five-hundred-thousand.

"Mom. I don't understand why I have to pretend to be someone that I'm not just because of my father's job. It's not like he's the prime minister. He just *works* for the prime minister. People don't care if the MoD's daughter dresses in black or has a nose ring."

"Yes, they do," she insists. "They notice and then your father has to field their questions. The Minister of Defense is a very important position to hold and people watch him. And when they see you acting like this, it's embarrassing."

I freeze and my eyes meet hers.

Fiery green gaze meets fiery green gaze.

"So, I'm an embarrassment?"

My mother freezes too and for a moment, I see uncertainty in her eyes, a hesitant waver. But then she steels herself again.

"Why wouldn't you be?" she demands harshly, all traces of the momentary softness gone. "You do everything you can possibly think of to embarrass us. And you do it on purpose. I don't know why you sound surprised. Yes, right now, you embarrass us."

I am quiet and still as I assess this. I never meant to embarrass them and it is a strange revelation. All I have ever wanted was to be left alone, left to dress how I want and act how I want. Is that really so much to ask?

Apparently so.

And it hits me like a brick wall.

I'm not going to win this argument.

I am suddenly overwhelmed by frustration and anger and a little hurt, too. So I swallow hard, then swallow again. Then I walk right past my mother without saying a word. As I walk through my bedroom door, I grip the heavy wooden edge in my fingers and slam it as hard as I can.

The walls shake.

And I am satisfied with that.

I calmly stroll down the hall leading away from my bedroom, ignoring the shocked expression on a nearby maid's face. Yes, we have maids. And butlers. And pool boys. No, I don't like it. But apparently, my opinion is about as important as Monopoly money is in the real world.

My mother comes barreling out of my room, just like I knew she would.

If she had guns, they would be blazing.

"Where do you think you're going? We do not slam doors in this house, young lady."

I just did. But I don't say that.

I am silent and mulish and I keep walking.

Mom tags along at my heels like a rat terrier, but I still keep walking. She grabs at my elbow and I shake her off. She falls behind and stays there.

"Just wait until your father comes home!" she calls.

I have to laugh at that.

It would be a terrifying threat, if in fact, my father comes home.

But he won't.

Because he seldom does.

I keep walking. I know that I'm being a spoiled bitch, but I can't see past my own annoyance at this point. This need of my mother's to force me into a perfect mold without any concern for my own wishes has come to a boiling point. I can't take it anymore.

I'm going to snap.

And maybe kill somebody.

And I won't look good in an orange jumpsuit.

Or actually, I probably would. I do look lovely in orange.

But that's beside the point.

I climb into my little red Mercedes convertible and jab at the button that slides the top down. There's nothing like the wind in my hair as I speed too quickly along Caberra's scenic highways. And I always, always speed too quickly.

I shift into first, then squeal my tires as I tear out of our curved semi-circle driveway. Mom ought to like that. She can just add it to her list of things that she's pissed off about.

I can hear her voice in my head right now. *Stanyos Giannis' daughter does not squeal her tires, young lady. You're an embarrassment.*

And then *I* am embarrassed when I suddenly realize that hot tears are welling up in my eyes.

Damn it. I wipe at them quickly.

I hate that I let her get to me like this. This should not have escalated into the feud that it has become. It's just a freaking nose stud. I can take it out and the hole will grow closed. It's not the end of the world. My mother, my father and in fact, the entire world, can eff off.

I shift into third, then fourth gear as I speed along the highway that leads to Valese, the capitol of Caberra. We live ten minutes outside of town, in a sleepy house where nothing happens.

Ever.

Except for a few screaming matches between my mother and father and me. And that seems to be happening more and more lately. It's probably mostly my fault, but I can't bring myself to conform to their stupid rules. Why should I have to? I'm not hurting anyone. Their stupid rules are stupid.

Asinine.

Ridiculous.

Pathetic.

The shoulder strap of my black tank top slips down and I yank it back up. I seriously wish that my best friend was here. But Reece went back to her home in Kansas for her senior year, taking another of my best friends, Dante Giliberti, with her. Dante's father is my father's boss, which makes Dante one of the few people in the world who knows exactly how I feel about these things. But he's gone now- a half a world away and I miss them both like crazy.

I fight the urge to pick up my phone and text Reece that very message. But these curves are too killer to text while driving. And I've already texted her that little message about 200 times since she left a month ago. It didn't change anything. They're still there and I'm still here.

Alone.

I can still feel my temper, right under the surface, boiling and hot. I've got to calm myself down. But I don't have anyone to talk to. Reece was my only real friend, besides Dante and Gavin. And Gavin is away until tomorrow on a trip with his dad.

I'm on my own, like usual.

And I'm pissed off at the world.

Like usual.

I sigh and maneuver my car through the busy streets of Valese. Before I can even think about it, I find myself driving toward the sea. My favorite place in the world. I love everything about it. The vastness, the saltiness, the beauty. I love the taste of it on my lips and the feel of the sea breeze in my hair. I love being here because I know that I will smell like the sea for hours after I leave. The water always seems to calm me down. So, before I even know it, I have parked my car and am standing with my toes in the water.

I'm not really sure how I got here.

Or why I am here.

But I'm happy that I am.

Caberra is beautiful. I have to give it that. An island nation just a stone's throw from Greece, it is gorgeous and tranquil and ancient. I wiggle my toes in the wet sand and enjoy how the cool water laps at my ankles. If it weren't daylight, I might just strip off my clothes and go skinny-dipping.

But it is.

Daylight.

So I don't.

Even I won't go that far.

My parents would freaking kill me.

Instead, I sit down and situate myself in the sand, keeping my toes in the water. I watch my black-glittery-toenail bob in and out of the current and I try to zone out, to forget my current angst with my mother.

I'm succeeding, too. That is, until a cowboy hat walks into my periphery.

No lie.

A cowboy hat.

In Caberra.

HolyFreakingHell.

I stop what I'm doing, the zoning out into a vegetative state, and stare. I can't help myself. We don't have cowboys in Caberra.

But apparently, we do now.

A giant of a man, or a boy, or a man-boy, is striding over the rolling sand dunes of the beach wearing cowboy boots and a cowboy hat. That is striking enough in its own right. But the muscles on this guy, the *guns*. His biceps look as thick as my thighs. Which, as a thigh, isn't that big. But as an arm! It's enormous.

I gulp, then stare at him again.

He's got sandy-blonde hair peeking from under his hat and what looks like dark brown eyes. He's wearing a button-up blue and white checked cowboy shirt with the arms ripped off and Levi's that look like they were created just for him.

Wow.

Just wow.

He's like a handsome alien creature here in Caberra, where the average guy wears board shorts and flip-flops and carries a surf board like it's an accessory. And it intrigues me. He looks like the kind of guy who is no stranger to hard labor and I bet a dollar to doughnuts that he's got calluses on his hands.

My heart flutters.

And so I imagine myself reaching in, wrapping my hands around it and squashing it like a bug.

Because a girl like me doesn't get all fluttery over a boy.

Any boy.

Not even the tough, good-looking ones.

And he is that.

Wow.

He hasn't noticed me yet. I don't know why, unless the brim of his cowboy hat impairs his vision. Although to be fair, he is momentarily distracted by a horseshoe crab.

I watch with interest as he kneels beside it and examines it, his face only a foot or so from the little beast. He acts like he's never seen one before as he reaches out a finger and tentatively pokes it. It lies still and I wonder briefly if it is dead and has been washed in by the current.

He pokes at it again, probably wondering the same thing.

And then the thing lurches into life, scuttling in a haphazard direction directly at man-boy. Man-boy jumps backward in surprise, landing directly on his chiseled backside in the wet sand. The crab continues scuttling toward him, probably disoriented, and man-boy continues to scramble backward, kicking at the crab.

In his cowboy boots.

I'm dying with laughter and I am not quiet about it.

This is literally the funniest thing I've seen in awhile.

Man-boy looks up and sees me laughing and glowers at me, which makes me laugh all the harder.

My bad mood has been lifted at the sight of this cowboy's boots digging into the sand trying to escape a harmless horseshoe crab. For that, I should thank him.

So I do.

I get to my feet, brush off the sand and make my way over to him. I offer him my hand, which he takes and I pull him to his feet.

He smiles and his grin is slightly crooked, which I actually find endearing. He's not gorgeous in a perfect way, he's gorgeous in an interesting way. He's got sexy stubble gracing his jawline and his eyes sparkle.

He is even better looking up close and I smile back.

"I'm Mia. And you're afraid of horseshoe crabs."

I speak in Caberran. Man-boy looks puzzled and holds his hands up.

"I don't speak Caberran," he says apologetically in English. So I repeat myself in English. He smiles again, crooked and mischievous.

"I'm Quinn. And no, I'm not. I'm not afraid of anything."

I start to laugh, then freeze.

"Quinn? As in, Reece's friend from Kansas?"

He grins again, cocky, self-assured.

"The very same. Quinn McKeyen. And you must be Mia, Reece's friend from Caberra. What a small world this must be."

He's got a charming American accent.

And I might die.

I've heard all about this guy. He's the one who Reece used to have a crush on, the guy who used to date Reece's friend Becca and who has come here to Caberra in the Foreign Exchange Student Program to live in Dante Giliberti's house.

I'm such an idiot. Whether or not I want to get all fluttery over him, I have to admit that his crooked grin is fairly panty-dropping. I can't crush on my best friend's old crush. *Can I?*

But as I stare at him, at this man-boy with the chiseled country-boy body, his crooked grin begs to differ.

He raises an eyebrow. "You are the same Mia, right?"

I nod, willing my voice to begin working again. What the eff is wrong with me?

"Yes. I am."

He nods, his cowboy hat dipping in an attractive way.

He's like a retro Marlboro commercial.

But younger.

And hotter.

Holy freaking cow.

"Well then. It's nice to meet you," he nods again and I notice that his eyes are warm and chocolately. I've always preferred blue eyes. But I am changing that stance as of right this minute. Brown is my new blue. I'm sure of it.

And then he turns around and walks away.

Wait.

Did that just happen?

I start to call after him, but then decide not to. I'm not going to be one of *those* girls, the kind that chases after a good-looking guy simply because they're good looking. And Quinn is definitely that.

Good-looking.

Very, very good looking.

Awesomely, amazingly good looking.

I watch his strong, wide shoulders sway as he disappears over the sand dunes.

And later, after I return home and go to bed, I dream about his milk-chocately stare.

Chapter Two

To: Reece Ellis > ReeciPiecie@thecloud.com
From: Mia Giannis > MiaAGiannis@maltanet.ma
Subject: HolyFreakingHotGuy

Reecie,
Soooooo. I met Quinn. Holyfreakinghell. You didn't tell me that he is so effing hot.
Shame on you. A girl needs some advanced warning for something like this.

-Mi

****

To: Mia Giannis > MiaAGiannis@maltanet.ma
From: Reece Ellis > ReeciPiecie@thecloud.com
Subject: Seriously?

Mi,
Seriously? You met him already? School hasn't even started.

But honestly, I had a crush on him for years—did you really think I'd crush on an ugly guy? Not hardly. Also, Dante is way hotter. Just saying.

XOXO,
Reecie

****

To: Reece Ellis > ReeciPiecie@thecloud.com
From: Mia Giannis > MiaAGiannis@maltanet.ma
Subject: Night and Day

Reece-

Dante's not better—Dante's just Dante. He's different from Quinn. Like night and day different. Quinn's got calluses and a cowboy hat and holyhell, his biceps! I've gotta go fan myself.

I'll have to talk to you later. How *is* Dante, anyway?

Love,
Mi

PS
Please come back soon. I miss you.

****

To: Mia Giannis > MiaAGiannis@maltanet.ma
From: Reece Ellis > ReeciPiecie@thecloud.com
Subject: I miss you too.

Mi,
I miss you, too. I think we're coming back for Christmas break.

And like you said, Dante is Dante. He can fit in anywhere.

Regarding Quinn, you should get to know him. There's a reason that I used to be so totally in love with him—he's a pretty good guy. I've known him since we were in diapers. And yes. He is hot.

XOXO,
Reecie

PS
What color are the stripes now?

****

To: Reece Ellis > ReeciPiecie@thecloud.com
From: Mia Giannis > MiaAGiannis@maltanet.ma
Subject: No joke.

Reecie,

No freaking joke. Tell me something I don't know.

Love,
Mi

PS
The stripes are blue.

I run my fingers through the blue streaks in my hair and sigh before I close my laptop. Life sucks without Reece and Dante here. This year will freaking suck without them here. Going to school will suck without them here.

But today's the day. And there's nothing I can do about it.

Except get my butt into gear and take a shower.

And get ready for the first day of school.

I sigh again.

Hell.

Chapter Three

The Piranhas are circling.

I watch them casually as my leg dangles from my open car door.

They are brightly colored, all with razor sharp teeth, all swarming in for the kill.

And they all have something in common. All of them think that they are better than everyone else because they have rich or important parents. Big deal. So do I. It's not all it's cracked up to be.

I should know. My life sucks.

In fact, I sort of hate my life.

Actually, not sort of. I do.

And I can't make myself get out and join them, not yet.

Because they might not be actual piranhas, but they may as well be.

The superficial girls are batting their eyes at cocky and arrogant boys, there is endless flirting and way too many noses in the air. Each one of those girls would stab me in the back quicker than they would even look at me. I know that. And it's all too much to deal with before breakfast.

Thankfully, the second bell hasn't even sounded, so I still have some precious alone time for just a few minutes more. I don't have to deal with these freaking barracudas yet.

"Hey Mia," a cheerful voice interrupts my solitude.

So scratch that. Alone time is over. But at least I haven't lost it to a barracuda.

"Hi Gavin," I turn and find Gavin Ariastasis.

As one of my best friends, I trust him because he's from the same exact position in life that I am in. Almost exactly. His father is Caberra's Minister of Interior, while mine is the Minister of Defense. Our lives are seriously effed up because of this. In fact, we might as well have our own little effed up club where we air out our own little effed up issues.

"Are you ready for our last year?" I ask absently, as I watch the fray in front of me. There's a certain first-day-of-school energy in the air today.

He laughs in response. Gavin is always laughing, actually. He's one of the happiest people I know. The world is a joke to him, a comedy, a play. And he's always in the center of the stage. But I like that about him. Everyone likes that about him. He doesn't take anything, including himself, too seriously.

"I'm ready for anything. Always," he announces to me.

One of the things I love the most about Gav is that he is so freaking cocky and self-assured. But he pulls it off in a likeable way, unlike most of these other cretins. That's why he's so likeable.

I laugh and stare up at him. He's good-looking in a very Caberran way. He's dark-haired, dark-eyed and carefree. And tan because he's always out in the sun. Like many of the other Caberran boys, he is a surfer. He was born to live in the sun. His eyes are almost always sparkling at some unsaid joke. But for some reason, I've never been attracted to him even though he's gorgeous. I don't know why because it would be so convenient.

But I guess hearts don't care about convenience.

"I see you've altered your uniform," he observes.

I glance down at myself. I have the blue plaid skirt on, the black knee socks and the white button-up shirt on like I should. But I've unbuttoned the top several buttons of my shirt and a black camisole peeks out. It's my homage to the rest of my wardrobe. Black, black, black. It fits my mood most of the time.

I even dye my hair jet black. Usually, much to my parents' chagrin, I add colorful streaks to it. Right now, as I told Reece, I have bright blue streaks. I figure I might as well coordinate with my school uniform.

I nod. "It's just a little thing."

A little tiny way to be an individual. But even a little of that kind of effort is considered too much around here.

Kolettis Academy does not exactly encourage individuality. It was founded by Antonio Kolettis, a Prime Minister from a few hundred years back, as the first private school in Valese. It is *the* private school now. Only the very rich, the very influential or the very powerful can get their kids in.

It's ironic that I spend my days day-dreaming about getting *out*.

But then, I'm contrary like that. Or so my parents say.

Gavin nods. "Just a little thing," he agrees. "Just a little thing that Kanaris might send you home for."

He does have a point. The headmaster, Constantine Kanaris, does not deviate from the rules. Not for any reason, not at any time. It's exhausting. But it's a little bit fun to play with. He can't expel me. My father is the MoD of our entire country.

But that doesn't mean that Kanaris won't send me home to change. He's done it before, many times. He only *wishes* that the policy had some specifications about hair color. But it doesn't. So I can color my head like the rainbow if I choose to.

Take that, asshole.

Gavin holds out his arm. "Come on," he urges me. "You can't stay out here all day."

I stare up at him. "I can't?" I ask. "Are you sure?"

He grins. And entire countries could be leveled with that charming grin, I am sure. And once again I ponder why I'm not attracted to him. It's probably because I've seen him in diapers. That tends to squash sex appeal.

"You can't," he reiterates cheerfully.

I sigh.

Then sigh again for good measure, just to make sure he heard me. Then I grab my bag, slam my car door shut and finally take Gavin's arm.

"Okay, fine," I tell him. "Let's get it over with."

He stares down at me, his dark gaze twinkling. "Well, when you put it so charmingly, how can I resist?"

I roll my eyes and he laughs. It's the story of our lives. I'm the sarcastic one with the dry wit, he's the endlessly happy one.

One foot in front of the other.

That's what I tell myself as we wind our way through the throngs of chattering kids and into the halls of our school.

One foot in front of the other and then before I know it, the day will be over and I'll be back home. Which will be miserable too, but not as miserable as school.

I hate my life.

It's official.

"So, have you heard from Dante?" Gavin asks me as we stand in line to receive our locker numbers.

I shake my head. "Not this week. But I got an email from Reece this morning. They don't start school until next week. Luckies."

"I don't know if they're so lucky," Gavin says as he drops me off at my locker. "Apparently, Kansas is hotter than Hades right now. And dusty. I got an email from Dante a couple of weeks ago. He said he's never seen so much dust outside of a desert."

"I would feel sorry for him, but... I don't," I say firmly. "He chose to go there. He could be here with us. It was his own decision."

Gavin looks at me with amusement. "I don't think he's feeling sorry for himself," he tells me. "He's pretty happy. I think he'd be happy anywhere Reece is, though."

I know that's right. If anyone was made for each other, even while being complete and total opposites, it is Dante and Reece. I can't help but wonder how smooth, polished Dante Giliberti is fitting into a rural Midwestern American school. But then I put the thoughts aside. Dante can handle any situation. He was bred for it. I'm sure he's totally fine.

Me, on the other hand...

I look around.

I'm surrounded, completely and totally, by kids that I can't stand.

Heaven help me.

I put my stuff into my locker except for my Trig book and slam it closed. Whoever gave me Trig for my first class of the day, before I've even had an ounce of caffeine, ought to be shot.

Right after they are drawn and quartered.

With those charming thoughts in my head, I make my way toward class and slide into a seat by the window.

One thing about Kolettis Academy, is that it is very, very nice. We have state of the art equipment, top notch teachers and the very best of everything, all situated in an ancient, beautiful building. We still use the original stone school building, although the interior has been fully remodeled several times throughout the years. The windows are large and allow me to fully see outside, to get a perfect view of the beauty that I am missing this morning. I can see the sea from here, I hear the sea gulls flying overhead and I can hear the water. It makes me sigh. Because I'm not there.

I'm here.

In prison.

"Miss Giannis?"

Uh-oh. Mr. Priftis' tone leads me to believe that it's not the first time he's called for me.

"Yes?"

I turn my attention to him.

"Are you awake, Miss Giannis?"

Luckily, Mr. Priftis seems amused. I nod quickly. "Yes, sir."

"Very well," he smiles. "I need you to share your textbook with Mr. McKeyen until I am able to order him one."

My heart lurches into my throat as I notice that Quinn, the one and the same, is seated next to me. He is all sprawled out, somehow fitting his large body into the smallish desk. How had I not noticed him arriving in this classroom? It's such a small room for such a big body.

My startled gaze is snared by his and I find amusement there. *Calm down*, I tell myself. *He can't read your thoughts.*

Or can he?

The amused expression on his face almost makes me think that he knows exactly how flustered he is making me.

"Miss Giannis?"

Mr. Priftis is less amused now and more concerned, his forehead wrinkled.

"Yes," I answer quickly. "Of course he can share my book."

"Excellent," Mr. Priftis answers as he returns to his desk. I turn to Quinn, Mr. RodeoGodHimself.

"If you scoot your desk over, you'll be able to see," I tell him.

Quinn extracts himself carefully from the desk and moves it, then sprawls out once again, but this time right next to me. I can smell him now, that freshly showered man smell and my stomach quivers.

I'm annoyed with myself.

I *do not* react like this to a guy. Not ever.

Quinn grins lazily at me and my stomach quivers again.

GodBlessIt. Freaking traitorous stomach.

And I realize that he's not wearing his hat. Probably because it's against school rules to wear a hat on the premises. His hair is definitely sandy blond and it curls up slightly at the nape of his neck. It's also slightly unruly, but I suspect that's a good reflection of his personality. Unruly. Rebellious. Ornery.

His white button-up shirt is slightly loosened at the top and his navy blue tie is not quite straight. He's wearing his boots and they are currently crossed at his ankles. He manages to look casual and sexy in this sterile classroom setting. I decide it must be an art.

"I like the stripes," he tells me, his dark eyes twinkling.

I stare at him for a moment until I realize that he means my hair. And before I can stop myself, I self-consciously run my fingers through a blue tendril.

"Thank you," I answer. I have no idea if he meant the compliment or if he was just using it as a way to point out that he noticed.

"You're very coordinated," he adds, gesturing toward my school uniform. I flush now. Because now he's teasing me.

I roll my eyes at him.

"What?" he asks innocently. But I can tell from his grin that he is anything but innocent. I flush again.

He looks at me quizzically, but Mr. Priftis starts his lecture and I turn my attention to him. It's difficult to ignore Quinn McSexy sitting next to me, particularly when I can feel his soft breath on my arm at times.

I gulp.

He smiles.

I die.

He winks.

He should look completely out of place. Because he *is* out of place even though he's wearing a uniform like everyone else, although his boots completely add a note of uniqueness to his outfit.

"Do you own any other shoes?" I whisper to him.

He stares down at me.

"Of course. I own football cleats."

"We don't play American football here," I tell him.

He looks chagrined.

"I know. They didn't tell me that before I came here though."

I'm sitting next to an American cliché. A big, muscular, hometown football hero, probably.

To satisfy my curiosity, I ask, "Did you play quarterback?"

Because that would be the ultimate cliché.

But he shakes his head.

"No. I play full-back."

I have no idea what that is, but I nod as though I do.

And then the bell is ringing and I am grabbing my books, saved from having to pretend that I know something about a topic that I actually know nothing about.

As everyone bustles into the hall, Quinn is surrounded by people trying to talk to him. He is new here; a curiosity, a distraction. *New* always equals *interesting*, at least for awhile. And I find myself feeling jealous when I see a throng of other girls milling about him.

I saw him first.

I can't stop the uninvited territorial feeling from welling up inside of me. As if I know him and have a claim to him. And then I shake it away. He's not mine. That's ridiculous. He's not anyone's. He's a stranger here, just trying to fit in and get through his senior year in a strange and foreign place.

But Quinn stands a head taller than most people and as he turns his head, his gaze meets mine. And there is something there, a familiar pull, almost like he is clinging to me from across the hall because he is surrounded by strangers and he feels like he knows me.

But he doesn't.

And I don't know him.

So I break his gaze and walk away.

And I am surprised by how hard it is to do.

Chapter Four

From: Reece Ellis > ReeciPiecie@thecloud.com
To: Mia Giannis > MiaAGiannis@maltanet.ma
Subject: First day?

M,

So how was your first day?? Did you see Quinn? How is he fitting into life on Caberra? I bet he sticks out like a sore thumb. I can sympathize, though. I was the same way.

It's hot here. Really, really freaking hot. Dante understands now why I call it Hell's Kitchen. School here starts next week, so Dante and I are school shopping today. I told him that he can't wear slacks here to school if he wants to fit in. But honestly, I can't picture him in Levi's, either. I'll take pics though and send them to you so you can see. It might be hi-lar-ious.

He came over yesterday and helped us throw hay bales. OMG. Regardless of what I tell him, he truly can fit in anywhere. My grandpa loves him.

I love you bunches and I miss you.

XOXO,
Reecie

My heart warms up as I read her message. I love that girl. She's my very first BFF and it doesn't matter that she's halfway across the world. But Christmas seems like a lifetime away right now.

I sigh and close my laptop.

I miss them both so much I can hardly stand it.

And now I'm being pathetic again.

I can't seem to help it. Since my parents are always so wrapped up in their political and social bullshit, and they don't allow me to hang around with anyone who isn't "appropriate", my circle of support is very limited. Dante, Reece and Gavin are all I have.

And that's not really that pathetic, I decide.

Because everybody needs somebody. No one is an island.

Right?

As if on cue, my cell phone buzzes from the pocket of my jeans which are in a pile on the floor. I reach from my bed and scoop it up.

"Gav?"

"How'd you know it was me?"

I can hear him smiling through the phone. And his eyes are probably sparkling. But that's a safe bet, because they're always sparkling. Gavin is always amused by something.

"I'm magic," I say glibly. "See, there's this cool new thing *technology*. I can see a person's phone number when they call."

"You're hilarious, do you know that?" Gavin grins again. Even though I can't see it, I know. I can't help but smile back, even though he can't see me.

"I know," I tell him. "What's up?"

"Nothing," he answers. "Just thought you might want to hang out today. Want to go diving?"

The answer to that question is almost always yes.

Day or night.

I love scuba diving or snorkeling or pretty much anything that involves me swimming beneath the surface of the sea.

Today is no different.

"Sure thing," I tell him. "I'll meet you at the pier in half an hour."

Which might be tricky since I'm supposed to be grounded for mouthing off to my mother the other day about my stupid nose ring.

Hmm. Quandary.

I'll have to put some thought into this.

But then I give up thinking about it and just leave.

What are they going to do to me? Take my birthday away?

I think not.

As I speed toward the beach, I do ponder the fact that I've been such a bitch lately. And for just a moment, I feel bad for my mom. She's left alone most of the time, trying to fulfill the duties of a political wife. I might sit down and have a talk with her when I get back.

Might.

If she doesn't kill me for leaving the house.

Which is unlikely.

So if I'm still alive when I get back, I might talk to her.

I nose my car into a parking spot and grab my gear. I'm so looking forward to this. There is nothing better for forgetting all of your problems than sinking below the surface of the sea where there is nothing but blue and solitude.

As I cross the boardwalk pier, I spot Gavin pulling on his wetsuit on the stern of his small boat, *The Shining.* The large motorboat was a sixteenth birthday gift to him from his parents and he named it because of his weird obsession with an old American movie of the same name.

I can still remember popping popcorn and watching it with him over and over when we were in junior high. I'll never forget Jack Nicholson's creepy face as he peeked in the door of the creepy hotel. Ugh. I had nightmares for weeks.

Gavin might have issues buried behind his ever-present grin.

Who else would be that obsessed with such a strange movie?

I smile at him though and hop aboard, dropping my bag on the seat next to him.

He gives me a quick hug and the rubber of his suit sticks to my skin.

"Hey, Mi," he says easily. "Check out the current today."

I glance at the horizon and the waves are pretty tall, at least two to three feet.

"Is there a wind advisory?" I ask, not worried, but curious.

He shakes his head. "Not yet," he tells me. "But we'd better hurry up and get out of the bay before there is."

I have to smile. He wants to hurry up and get out of the bay before the harbor master can tell him that it's too dangerous to go out today. Seriously, Gavin has no fear. He always just assumes that things will be okay. And I guess that's something that he and I share.

I usually feel the same way.

Things will always turn out okay because they always have.

Even this summer, when there was an assassination attempt on Dante's father and Dante himself was caught up in the same mess, everything turned out okay. And if something like that can work itself out, then pretty much anything else can work out too.

I know.

Skewed logic.

"Well, let's hurry up then," I tell Gavin.

He grins his ornery grin. "Just as soon as our guest arrives," he answers, glancing at his watch. "He should be here any minute."

"Guest?" I raise an eyebrow.

"Yeah," Gavin answers. "The new guy. I felt sorry for him- he doesn't know anyone here."

"Oh." I feel like somebody kicked me in the stomach and I don't know why. "Reece's friend."

I have undefined feelings for this guy. I can't decide if I like that he gets my heart going or if I hate it. So right now, I'm reserving the right to decide later. Honestly, that's better than my usual gut instinct to hate everything.

And in the meantime, I'll just enjoy looking at him.

"Right," Gavin nods. "Reece's friend. He seems nice enough."

"Well, Reece always says that people from the American Midwest are the friendliest in the world," I answer absently. My eyes are glued to the pier, watching for Quinn.

Gavin notices.

"Do you mind that I invited him?"

I don't know why he sounds surprised. I'm not exactly what you would call a people person. It usually takes me a little while to warm up to someone.

"No, of course not," I say anyway. "It's your boat. You can invite anyone you'd like. Except Elena, of course."

Gavin laughs at this. Elena Kontou is the notorious Mean Queen of our class. Her mother is in Dimitri Giliberti's Cabinet which has always put her into our select little group. But she's mean as a snake even though she has a perfect face.

Actually, make that *had* a perfect face.

Her cheek was scarred in the same yacht explosion that injured Dimitri Giliberti this past summer. She's had a couple of surgeries to correct it, but you can still see it. And she sort of blames me, because my sort-of-boyfriend at the time, Vincent, was the one who rigged the yacht to explode.

Have I mentioned that my life is complicated?

Yeah.

It is.

But now Vincent is waiting for his trial and Elena's face is still scarred. And she has to have someone to blame. And I'm it.

Lucky me.

"Okay," Gavin agrees. "I will never invite Elena when you're here."

"You'd invite her otherwise?"

I am shocked by this notion.

"She's a snake, Gav. And she can't swim. You shouldn't take her out on the water with you."

He starts to say something, but we're interrupted by an American drawl.

"I'm not a snake, but I can't swim either. Is that a problem?"

I look up to find the tips of two battered cowboy boots poking over the edge of the pier.

Quinn's gaze meets mine and I find that he is completely unembarrassed by this.

"You seriously can't swim?" I ask, sure that he is kidding. "Everyone can swim."

"No, they can't," he answers easily as he hops into the boat. "Apparently, the snake and I can't. Hey, dude," he greets Gavin. "Thank you again for the invite. I was going crazy at Giliberti House. I was starting to talk to myself."

"No problem," Gavin slaps his shoulder and hands him a life jacket. "You'd better wear this if you really can't swim."

Quinn takes off his shirt and I am instantly distracted by this.

HolySweetMotherOfGod.

What do they feed the boys in Kansas?

This guy is built like a lean brick house. I can easily count his ab muscles and they ripple every time he moves.

Holy. Cow.

He straps on the bright orange life jacket and looks down at me.

"See something you like?"

And now he's cocky.

And I like it.

What is wrong with me that I like cockiness as a character trait?

I shake my head and lie. "Nope. Nothing in particular."

He grins, unabashed. "Whatever you say."

His expression is knowing. And annoying.

"Look, farmboy. I know that you're Mr. Hometown Football Hero back home, but here, you're not. So, you should start out your relationships with a little less ego. People will like you more."

"Hmm," he says, staring at me thoughtfully. "Kitten has claws."

Gavin is staring me in complete and utter surprise. I'm not usually so bitchy and to be honest, I don't know what came over me. I shake my head and look away from both of them. Gavin takes the wheel and we're gliding our way out onto open water. Only now, the silence is sort of uncomfortable.

And it's my fault.

"Look," I turn to Quinn. "I'm sorry. I'm not that good with new people."

"Really?" he answers innocently with that lopsided grin. "I hadn't noticed."

Gavin busts out laughing and I have to laugh too.

"I'm really sorry," I say again. "I guess I have trust issues with new people. It seems like so often they just want something from me. But I know that's not the case with you."

He eyes me up and down. And then leans in to murmur into my ear.

"Don't be so sure."

And my cheeks are instantly flushed.

OhMyWord.

Did he really just mean what I think he meant?

My eyes meet his and he nods, as if he could hear my unspoken question.

I'm starting to feel like he can read my freaking mind.

And I'm still blushing.

So I ignore him.

And my racing heart.

Good lord.

We race from the bay and out into open water while the waves toss *The Shining* about. We probably shouldn't be out here, but the dangerousness of it gives it a more exciting edge.

We're probably insane.

Gav looks at me. "Do you want to go out to the wrecks or stick to the reef?"

Either way, we'd be insane. The wrecks, a collection of old sunken ships, are quite a ways from the bay and the waves will be crazy big there today. And the reef… well, let's just say that sharks enjoy the reef. A lot.

"Wrecks," I say.

"Done," he grins.

He turns the boat into that direction and the wind blows my hair from my face.

I notice that Quinn is gripping the side pretty hard. So hard, in fact, that his fingers are white. Interesting. Is the Hometown Hero afraid of boats?

And then I feel bad for thinking of him as Hometown Hero. I decide that I will ask Reece about that before I do it again. I might be way off base, but I doubt it.

I turn my attention away from both of the guys onboard and instead, stare out at the water. I was right. The waves here are huge. No wonder Quinn is nervous. He's not used to the sea at all. And he can't swim. And since that's the case, I decide that he must be pretty brave to come out onto the sea in these waves in a little motorboat.

Or maybe stupid. I haven't decided yet.

I lean over and put my hand on his arm for a minute.

"Don't worry," I tell him with a grin. "I won't let you drown."

He raises an eyebrow.

"How would you save me, Tiny Tot? You're half my size."

And that is a true statement.

I eye him, at the way he is once again sprawled out, casually fitting himself into the boat seat.

"How tall are you, anyway?" I ask.

"6'6," he answers. "I ate my spinach when I was growing up."

Holy crap. I practically *am* half his size. He's gigantic.

He leans over to me.

"And I wear size 14 shoe. Do you know what they say about the size of a man's foot?"

My cheeks flare into color.

Yes, I've heard of the saying.

The size of a man's foot is supposed to be directly parallel to the size of his... um, male unit.

I can't even help myself.

I eye his foot.

And it is gigantic.

My eyes fly to his face and find that he is nodding again. And then he laughs.

Gavin is shaking his head. He's never seen me blush so much. That much is true. I'm usually unflappable. But this guy. He gets to me.

And I've almost decided that I hate it.

But the verdict is still out.

Because I might like it.

Gavin drops anchor and the waves really are crazy. The boat is rolling on top of them and I have a brief sense of hesitation.

"Should we stay out here?" I ask him hesitantly.

He looks at the water and shrugs.

"We're here now. Let's just take a quick dive and then we'll head in."

I nod. "Fine with me."

I pull my wet suit on over my bathing suit and slide the mask onto my face. Gavin lifts the oxygen tank onto my back.

Quinn watches us prepare.

"Is there anything I should be doing?" he asks.

Gavin shakes his head. "Nope. The boat is anchored, so you won't go anywhere. We'll be back up shortly."

Quinn nods and Gavin grabs my hand and we jump over the side without hesitation.

It is instantly calm beneath the water.

It is exactly why I love to dive.

Nothing can reach us here in the quiet underwater world. No troubles, no stress, no worry.

My flippers slide through the water with ease, propelling me downward. My hands cut through the crystal blue water and Gavin is right beside me. I glance upward and I can still see the outline of the boat above. It looks like a giant whale from here.

I turn my attention back to the water below me.

I can just see the moss-covered tip of a mast of a sunken galleon when a strange sensation ripples through my body. I stop moving and the sensation grows.

It's a rumbling vibration, a weird shaking.

It's literally rolling through my body, like I'm sitting in a car with the bass turned up too loud.

I look at Gavin, my eyes wide. He is frozen too, floating in place in the water.

Our eyes meet.

And then we notice that the sandy sediment on the sea floor is rolling toward us in murky billows.

What the eff?

The water continues to vibrate and shake around us and the moment that I think the word *shake*, it occurs to me.

Earthquake.

Chapter Five

Gavin realizes it at the same moment that I do and we both spin and propel ourselves upwards.

HolyEffingEarthquake.

I burst from the surface of the water and grip the side of the boat and I can still feel the rumbling in the sea. In order for us to feel it all the way out here, the earthquake must be enormous. We haven't had a big one in years and years, way before my lifetime.

Gavin pulls himself over the side and then reaches over to give me a hand. I land on the floor of the boat in a clumsy heap and instantly start pulling off my stuff. My flippers, wetsuit and oxygen tank land in a pile.

"What's going on?" Quinn asks. He can see the anxiety on our faces and I'm sure he can see the vibrating water.

"Earthquake," Gavin tells him. Gav isn't even undressing, he's turning the boat toward shore in his flippers, guiding the boat with capable hands.

Quinn looks startled and he stands up to look out at the horizon. But the rough water knocks him back down. He sprawls in a seat and stares at me in shock.

My heart thumps in my chest.

This isn't good.

And from the look on Gavin's face, the dead-serious expression that he never, ever gets, he knows it too. We're right in the middle of a serious situation, maybe even dire.

I gulp.

As we race toward the shore, jumping hard over waves, my teeth jar every time we land. We hit the water so hard that I can't believe the belly of the boat doesn't splinter into pieces. I grit my teeth and hold on.

Quinn is silent now and I almost wonder what he's thinking, but then I'm distracted by trying to hold on to the things that keep trying to fly out of the boat, like life preservers, bags, flippers and so on. I've never seen the current or waves so bad.

We fly into the bay and the way the boats are rolling on the waves as they sit in their slips is unnerving. They are haunting and spooky as they move with the sea. One of them has flipped onto its side and I know that it will sink. Water is flooding its deck. Debris is floating in the water; oars and cushions and cups and pieces of wood, and I am almost too afraid to look onto the shore.

But I do.

And I gasp.

The Harbor Master's building is in rubble, in an absolute shambles.

And the complete seriousness of this hits us.

"Holy shit," Gavin breathes. He reaches over and grabs my hand as he noses us into his slip. "We've got to move."

"But where should we go?" I ask as we scramble from the boat and onto dry land. The ground is not moving, but after a moment, I feel a short rumble.

Aftershocks.

They vibrate my feet and I gulp.

Even the air feels scary, like a premonition or foreboding. Or something. I try to ignore it.

"I don't know," Gavin admits. He climbs up beside me, then releases my hand to help Quinn from the swaying boat. "Somewhere other than here."

"We should stay together," Quinn points out calmly.

He's right. And I say so.

There's no one else in the harbor, something that I find strange. Although, looking back, I realize that there wasn't really anyone here when we left. Everyone else was smart enough to not venture into the waves.

Gavin's cell phone rings and we look at each other, startled.

In the heat of the moment, we had forgotten that we had phones.

He picks it up and I can see the relief on his face as he talks to his mom. After a few moments, he hangs up and looks at me.

"My parents are fine. But the Earthquake was bad. Roads are blocked. My parents say to go to the Old Palace and wait there."

I gulp.

With shaking fingers, I pull out my phone. I try my house and there is no answer. I try again, and this time, I get a weird busy signal.

This can't be good.

"Gavin, I've got to go to my house," I tell him.

He looks uncertain. "But my parents said we should wait at the Old Palace. I'm sure yours would want you to do the same thing. Your father is probably there."

The Old Palace is the Capitol building of Caberra. It houses the courts, various government agencies and the Prime Minister's residence and it is where our fathers work. It is located in the heart of Valese and it is in the exact opposite direction of my house from here.

Quinn steps forward. "Surely we can drive past Mia's house on the way to the Old Palace," he says. "It's only a little out of the way, right?"

I am grateful for this. I am shaken and scared and it's nice to have someone back me up. Although, I'm fairly certain that Gavin would have taken me anyway. He nods reluctantly now.

"Okay. If the roads are passable. We have to watch for downed power lines, though. We don't want to get electrocuted."

I gulp again. I have the feeling this is going to be a national disaster.

As we walk to Gavin's car, a large black Land Rover, I try to call my house again. I get the weird busy signal again.

A heavy feeling settles in my stomach.

Something isn't right at my house.

I know it right now.

We drive in silence and from the passenger seat, I stare at the carnage from my window. Houses are in rubble everywhere. Beautiful ancient buildings and shiny modern ones too.

This can't be happening.

But it is.

Sirens wail and the entire scene seems to pass by in slow motion. I know it is because I'm in shock. And anyone would be in shock. Gavin seems to be, too. Quinn is quiet in the backseat and we watch people walking aimlessly. Everyone seems astounded. People are dirty, their clothing torn.

Our home country is a wreck.

"It's probably a good thing we were on the water," Gavin says quietly. "We weren't in a building somewhere."

And then it hits me.

My parents don't know where I am.

I'm supposed to be in my room, but I left.

I left without telling them.

My heart lodges in my throat and the guilt is unbearable.

We are able to drive through the carnage and reach my house. But when we get to the electric gates, they won't open when I punch in the code. And I realize that there must not be any power.

"Can you give me a boost?" I ask Quinn. He looks surprised.

"You want to climb over that?" He eyes the tall brick wall. "How will you get back over?"

I shrug. "I'll figure out how to push the gate open."

"I'm coming with you," he says firmly, as he cups his hands for me to step into. I'm surprised, because he doesn't know me or owe me anything. But I don't say anything. I step into his hands and he vaults me over the wall. He quickly follows me, and Gavin after him. The three of us make our way up my long driveway and I can't believe my eyes.

My house is in rubble.

Trees are down everywhere on the property and it truly looks like a warzone.

This.

Can't.

Be.

Happening.

Everything is still and silent. And then there is another rumbling aftershock and I can't help but gasp. The sound is noisy in the silence.

This is freaking insane. My crumbled house is like an eerie ghost town.

"It's going to be fine," Quinn tells me quietly. His presence is calming. I hadn't noticed that before, but it is true. "I promise."

"How can you promise that?" I ask him. "You don't know."

"I do know." He nods confidently.

But I don't feel so confident.

Everything is spookily calm and quiet. I don't see my mom or even the servants, which is odd. It's only been half an hour since the quake. This causes a heavy feeling to lodge in my throat. Where are they?

I push through the rubble of my front door and find that everything is knocked down in my house. The walls, the ceiling, the doors. Wires are hanging haphazardly, chandeliers look hauntingly gaunt and skeletal as they hang limply in the air.

"Mom?" I call out. My voice seems small in this silent chaos.

"Adrianna?" Gavin yells.

No answer.

I plow forward, pushing broken and jagged things out of my way.

Quinn grabs my arm.

"Be careful," he warns me. "There could be exposed wires."

I gulp.

Then continue on.

My mom would have looked for me in this mess. She wouldn't have left, because she would think that I was under the rubble in my room. Because my room is where I'm supposed to be.

My heart is heavy as I head down what is left of the hallway leading to my room.

There is no noise here but for the crackle and pop of debris.

"Mom?" I call again, but my voice doesn't contain any hope. Because if my mother is here, she is unable to answer and I don't want to speculate on why that might be.

"Mia," Gavin says uncertainly as the building rumbles and moans around us. "We shouldn't be here. This isn't safe."

Even as he speaks, a piece of the hallway wall tumbles in front of us and Quinn yanks me out of the way.

"Let's go," Gavin urges me. His eyes are anxious.

"Just a minute," I insist. "I just have to look inside of my room. That's where she would have gone."

"You have one minute," Gavin says firmly. I nod and he stays right on my heels. Quinn still has my elbow. And everything is a blur.

I'm numb as I creep into the wreckage that used to house all of my most precious and personal things. Everything is in a mess now, all broken and torn and dirty. My bed is nonexistent. My clothing is scattered on the floor. I can't even fathom how strong this earthquake must have been to have done this much damage.

"Mom?" I call again.

I climb over bricks that used to be walls and stumble on what is left of my bed.

I pull myself up onto my hands and knees and peer over what seems to be a mountain of wreckage.

And then the earth quakes again.

It rumbles, low and loud, and I hear several pops and cracks from beneath me.

I don't know if it is a strong aftershock or another earthquake, but I hear Gavin yell and feel someone yank my arm right before there is a sharp pain in my temple and my vision explodes into a bright white light.

And then there is nothing at all.

Chapter Six

Something is annoying me.

This is my first thought because it takes me a moment to place what it is.

Something is moving. It's disturbing me, waking me.

And then I realize that it's my own finger.

It's moving on its own accord, twitching against the side of my leg.

I try to open my eyes, but my eyelids feel heavy and tired, like they have been glued closed. I try again and then again, and finally, finally, they open.

Slowly.

And the light hurts my eyes.

I can't focus.

Everything looks like blurry shapes and fuzzy outlines and I blink, trying to clear things up. It doesn't help. I blink again and it is so incredibly, frustratingly hard. My eyes don't want to cooperate. After a few minutes, I finally bring things into a slightly clearer focus, but it's not perfect.

But it's enough to see a figure sitting in a chair by the window.

It's a woman.

Her head is bowed and I think she is asleep.

I have no idea where I am.

"Mia!"

She wasn't asleep. The figure jumps to her feet and lunges to my side. Her face is anxious, frantic, hopeful. I stare at her in confusion.

Because I don't know her.

And then I realize something else.

I don't know *me*.

Alarm slams into me, causing me to panic.

"Who are you?" I ask her wildly. "Where am I?"

This can't be happening because I don't know who I am. My heart is speeding, pulsing, threatening to burst.

HolyHell.

HolyHell.

HolyHell.

I grab her hand and look into her eyes. They are green and startled and instantly concerned.

"Who are you?" I beg her.

A tear drops from the corner of her eye.

"I'm your mother," she answers uncertainly and she reaches for the call button. She presses it, but then runs for the door, calling for a nurse. And then she stops at a sofa on the way back to my bed, and she shakes someone's shoulder.

And I realize that someone is lying there. A man. And I didn't even see him before. I wipe at my eyes and realize that they are covered in goop. I wipe at them again and my vision clears a little.

The man approaches me with *my mother*, the mother that I don't remember and don't know, and he looks concerned. He's tall and dark and has silver at his temples.

And I don't know him, either.

"Mia," he begins. "Do you know who you are? Do you remember what happened?"

I'm panicky again. It feels like butterflies are banging their wings against my ribcage, trying to get out. I don't blame them. I want to get out too.

"No," I answer uncertainly. "Who are you?"

"I'm your father," the strange man answers calmly. But he is interrupted by a nurse who comes through the door. When she sees that I am awake, she approaches me quickly, checking my pulse and looking into my eyes. She wipes the rest of the goop away and now I can see.

My mother is crying and telling the nurse that I don't know her.

And the nurse looks at me.

"Do you know who you are?" she asks gently.

I shake my head and my mother cries harder.

"Do you remember anything that happened?" the nurse asks.

I shake my head again.

"It's alright," she tells me and she pats my hand. "Everything will be alright."

Will it?

Because my parents are standing next to me and I don't seem to remember them. And I don't remember me, either.

And I don't see how in the world that can be alright.

I'm getting very, very panicky.

A doctor comes in a few minutes later. He pokes and prods at me, too, in all the same places as the nurse.

He looks into my eyes and listens to my heart and nods.

"I hear that you don't remember very much," he tells me. I nod.

"Don't worry," he tells me. "You've suffered a head injury. Your brain was swollen and you were placed in a medically induced coma to protect you. We reduced your medication yesterday and you woke up on your own accord today. Physically, you are fine, so do not worry about that."

"Why can't I remember anything?" I whisper.

The doctor's eyes are kind.

"Because you've had a trauma," he tells me. "As the swelling continues to decrease, your memory may come back. As time passes, it may come back that way too. Memory loss as a result of brain trauma is a tricky thing. But you are surrounded by people who love you and I have confidence that you will be fine."

I swallow hard and my throat is sore. The doctor notices me wincing.

"You had a breathing tube," he tells me. "You might notice some tracheal tenderness for a day or two."

Tracheal tenderness. That sounds so medical.

I am still for a moment. My memory is a strange thing. As I think, I can remember bits and pieces of things. I see a car. A red convertible. I think it's mine, but it might not be. I see a boat. I see underwater murkiness. But there is nothing else.

I look at my mother.

"I'm sorry that I don't remember you," I tell her politely.

She cries.

"Adrianna," my father says sternly. "Mia doesn't need this right now." He pats her back awkwardly and I note that. My father isn't great with affection, apparently. "You need to be strong."

She nods, but she's still crying.

"What is my full name?" I ask my father. He looks slightly pained.

"Mia Alexandria Giannis," he tells me. The name doesn't mean anything to me. Nothing at all. It doesn't feel like me. But then again, I don't know me.

"Your middle name is after my mother," he adds. "Your grandmother. You are very much like her. Very strong-willed and independent."

Strong willed?

I wonder about this. I don't feel strong willed right this moment. I feel confused and tired. And weak. I don't like the feeling.

"You should rest," my father tells me. And I realize that I don't even know his name. So I ask and he looks pained again.

"It's Stanyos," he tells me. "Stanyos Alexander Giannis."

"After your mother?" I guess. He smiles and nods.

"Yes."

He's satisfied with me for some reason. I've done something right, but I don't know what. Maybe he's just proud of me that I woke up.

"What happened?" I ask. Because I realize that I have no idea what happened to put me into this condition.

"There was an earthquake," my mother pipes up. Her eyes are red from crying. "You were grounded. And you sneaked away to go scuba diving. But that's a good thing. If you'd been in your room like you were supposed to be when the quake happened, you might have been killed. For once, your rebelliousness was a good thing."

She sounds a little bitter and my father gives her a hard look.

"Adrianna."

She lowers her eyes and I know that I'm missing something. But I'm too tired to worry about it.

"So I like to scuba dive?"

My father smiles again.

"It's your favorite thing in the world."

That makes sense. I only have a handful of memories that I can recall and they involve the water. I tell them that. My father smiles, my mother does not. She seems very upset about something that I don't understand. But again, I'm too tired to make sense of it now.

I tell them this, that I am so very tired. And they tell me to get some sleep, that they aren't going anywhere.

So I close my eyes. But when you are a in a place that you don't know, with strangers watching your every move and when, in fact, you don't even know who you are... it is very hard to sleep.

But I'm going to give it the old college try.

And then I realize that I have no idea where that saying came from. Somewhere from the back recesses of my mind, probably.

I can tell already that this getting my memory back thing is going to be a long process.

Sigh.

Chapter Seven

Days pass in a blur of strange faces and visitors.

Apparently, all of my friends from school come to see me, all of the ones who weren't also injured in the earthquake. And I don't recognize any of them.

The strange thing is that I know what everything around me is. I know the television, the bed, the bathroom, my slippers. I recognize how those things work. It's like my memory has holes in it. I remember some things but everything else just dropped out of existence, like I never knew it at all. It's frustrating.

Also, apparently, I like red jello. It's pretty much all I want to eat right now. The meat on my tray makes me want to gag.

My mother sighs.

"Mia, you're not a vegetarian. You've never been a vegetarian. Just eat your food, alright? You need the strength and you're not going to get it from jello alone."

I stare at her.

"Maybe I should have been a vegetarian," I announce, laying my spoon down and putting the cover back over my tray. I don't even want to look at the greenish tinted hospital chicken. (Who in their right mind would eat that??) "And maybe I'll become one now."

"Mia," my mother sighs again. "What has gotten into you today? You're not normally like this.... so obstinate."

I stare at her again. I'm not? So, I don't usually have opinions? I must have been a very boring person. I'm prevented from responding by another visitor.

"Mia's being obstinate? How out of character," a dark-haired guy says wryly. He steps into the room and I wrack my brain. I was introduced to him a few days ago. Gavin. His name is Gavin. And we were- *are*- good friends.

Apparently.

"Hi Gavin," I tell him. I smile politely. It's hard to pretend to be good friends with someone that I don't remember. They all tell me that they understand, but there's no way that they can. I just hope that I don't accidentally hurt someone's feelings by forgetting them.

"Hey," Gavin tells me. He pulls up a chair next to me and I examine him. Dark hair, dark brown eyes, mischievous smile. Crisp white button-down shirt, open at the top, fancy blue jeans, flip-flops.

He's gorgeous. My tummy gets a little fluttery when he picks up my hand as if he knows me.

Then I remember, he *does* know me.

I just don't know *him*.

"How do you feel today?" he asks. "Are you driving the nurses crazy?"

"No, she is not," My mother says firmly, even though clearly the question was meant for me. "She's being polite and courteous, as she should be."

Gavin looks at me. There is confusion and a bit of amusement in his dark eyes, but he quickly masks it. He's good at this, at smoothing things over. I make a note of that.

"How are you feeling?" he asks again. He's still holding my hand and his fingers are warm. I like it. I may not know him, but I like his hand. "Have they let you outdoors yet for a walk?"

"Not yet," I tell him. "I feel good enough though."

"Then you shall go," he tells me valiantly. He picks up the call button and a moment later a nurse appears.

"Yes?" she asks pleasantly. Gavin smiles at her, with a knee-weakening grin.

"Miss Giannis would love to go for a walk in the sunshine," he says. "Would that be possible? I'll walk with her."

My gaze meets his and his eyes are sparkling. It's no wonder he and I were good friends. He's very likeable.

The nurse smiles at him. No one is impervious to his charms, apparently.

"She has already been cleared for a walk outside," the nurse tells him. "She just hasn't wanted to go."

Gavin turns to me. "No? Put your clothes on, Mia . We're going outside."

I stare at him. "I sort of don't want to."

"And why not?" he looks at me. "Because you'd rather lay in here and feel sorry for yourself?"

"No."

Yes.

Gavin raises an eyebrow. "No? That's not what I've been told."

I look to my mother and she appears guilty.

"You've been talking about me?" I ask softly. This actually hurts. I've been trying really hard this week—to do what everyone has asked of me. And she's been talking about me?

"No. Yes. I mean, I have, but only because I'm concerned about you," she stammers. "Gavin has always been able to cheer you up, so I called him."

I stare at her, but Gavin interrupts.

"I'm going to go outside for a minute, so get your clothes on. We're getting some fresh air."

"Have you always been this bossy?" I ask him. He grins.

"Why, yes. Yes, I have. And you like it." He saunters out, not worried in the slightest that I might actually be agitated with him.

My mother follows him out and I feel my temper bubbling just beneath the surface. But I tamp it down. I'm sure they're just concerned. Right?

Whatever.

I swing my legs over the side of the bed and sit for a second. Obviously, I've been out of bed here in the room to shower and use the bathroom and whatnot. But the idea of going outside, out into the hospital and into the world and the sunshine, has made me terrified.

I don't want to admit that to anyone because I feel silly.

But it's the truth.

I don't know if it's the accident, or if I've always been that way.

Who's to say?

Certainly not me.

I can't remember anything.

I pull on some clothing. A khaki skirt and a cream-colored blouse. A pair of tan ballet flats. These clothes feel foreign. I can't believe I would choose clothing so bland. And so...*beige*. But apparently, I did.

Apparently, I was a bland person.

And I use the word *apparently* a lot.

I pull a brush through my hair and stare in the mirror.

Dark brown hair, green eyes. I'm sort of small. Not small in a weird, misshapen way, but small, nonetheless. I guess I'm pretty, although I look a bit pale from being indoors. I probably should get some sun. Some vitamin D therapy might improve my attitude, too.

For some reason, I feel so agitated. My mother tells me that it's very unusual for me, that I'm usually a very cheerful person, but that a certain level of agitation is normal given the circumstances.

I don't know about that.

But then, I don't know about anything right now.

And I'm back to that again. Sigh.

I poke my head out into the hall and find my mother and Gavin talking to each other against the wall.

I fight back the feeling of annoyance that rises in me, the bad taste that is in my mouth.

What the eff?

If he's my friend, why is he in cahoots with my mother?

And where the heck did I get a word like *cahoots*?

Can't my friend talk to my mother? I'm clearly a lunatic. I wonder if I was before this accident, too, or if it's a new thing.

I'm shaking my head when they notice me.

Gavin smiles.

"Are you ready?"

His smile is a thousand-watt light-bulb and I relax. I'm being hypersensitive, I'm sure. That's probably normal, given the circumstances.

Gavin holds his arm out and they both smile at me.

And once again, I am uneasy, but don't know why.

"I'm ready," I confirm, as I slip my arms around his forearm. My mother falls back into my room as Gavin and I make our way down the hall and out of the hospital.

The sun hits me squarely in the face and I blink my eyes.

"You okay?" Gavin asks quietly. He has apparently noticed that my feet are now frozen to the ground and I am refusing to move from this spot.

"Yeah," I mumble. "I just feel intimidated by coming out here. I don't know why. It makes me feel sort of panicky."

I'm such a baby.

I look around, at the shrubbery in the hospital courtyard, at the benches filled with visitors and patients, at the flowers, the grass, at the wide open blue sky above us. And all I can do is to try and still my racing heart. I don't know why I'm so anxious about this place. It's irrational.

"You know," Gavin says quietly as he leads me around the path. "We were here last year. Our friend Dante had a car accident. And when we came here, we weren't sure exactly what we were going to find. We knew he was alive and they told us that he was okay, but we didn't really believe it until we saw it for ourselves. Maybe that's it. Maybe you have some suppressed memories deep down about that time. It was pretty emotional. It was one of the only times I've seen you cry."

I look at him. The sun is shining onto his face, illuminating his already bright smile. He's a gorgeous guy, that much is true. Strong, good-looking and self-assured. That's a good recipe for destruction.

"I don't cry?" I ask hesitantly. That doesn't seem right. Because right now, I feel like a blubbering mess on the inside. Gavin shakes his head.

"Not usually. You're pretty bad-ass."

I have to smile at that. "Bad ass?"

He nods. "Yup. Totally bad-ass."

"Tell me why you say that," I instruct him.

We continue walking around the pretty landscaped sidewalk as Gavin tells me escapades of my youth, beginning from the time we were in primary school. He speaks smoothly and calmly as we walk around patients who are walking slower than we are.

"And then there was the time that you got the assistant principal at school fired- when we were only in fourth grade. You thought he discriminated against you because he was a pacifist and your father was the minister of defense."

"*Did* he discriminate against me?" I ask, with my eyebrow raised.

Gavin nods. "It sure seemed like it."

"So, I'm ballsy."

Gavin laughs. "Yes, you're ballsy."

"Why are you and I such good friends? Have we always been? Have we ever dated?"

Gavin stares at me.

"You truly don't remember anything, do you?" he asks softly. There is sympathy in his eyes and I hate that. I'm not asking for sympathy. I'm just trying to learn more about myself.

"Don't feel sorry for me, Gav,"I tell him. "I don't need sympathy."

He stares at me again.

"You just called me Gav," he points out quietly. "I haven't told you that you used to do that."

I am instantly still. Holy crap. He's right.

"I don't know where that came from," I admit. "It just came out. It felt natural."

"It's your memory," Gavin decides confidently. "Subconsciously, in there somewhere, you know me." He grins. "Because seriously, dude, how could you truly forget *me?*"

He is cocky and arrogant and pleasingly so. I smile back.

"I don't know. It's like I got hit on the head or something. Oh, wait. I did."

He laughs and I laugh and it suddenly seems normal to hang out with him. Relaxed. Friendly. Normal. I'm digging it. So I tell him that.

He looks surprised.

"Did you doubt that you would?" He is cocky again. "Your favorite time of the day is always Gavin Time."

"Gavin Time?" I repeat doubtfully. "Are you always this sure of yourself?" I ask, one eyebrow cocked. He laughs. He tightens his grip on my elbow and I enjoy the feeling of his warm fingers on my skin.

"Always," he says, leaning in toward me like he's confiding something. "It's one of the things you love about me."

"So I love things about you, then?" I ask, laughing.

Gavin smiles. "Of course you do. Everyone does."

He winks and laughs and I laugh again.

"Have we ever had sex?" I ask. Gavin's head snaps back and he stares at me again, his eyes sparkling and appraising.

"Not yet," he says. "Would you like to?"

He nudges me and laughs, but now I'm on a mission to find out things about myself that my mother probably wouldn't know, so I ignore his charming grin.

"Am I a virgin?" I ask hesitantly. "Do you know?"

He stares at me yet again, but this time he actually seems uncomfortable. If it was possible to squirm while standing in an upright position, he'd totally be doing it. It makes me uneasy.

"What?" I ask. "Am I a slut?"

He rolls his eyes. "No. You're not a slut. Far from it. But you're not a virgin, either."

"But we haven't had sex?" I ask again. He winks.

"Not yet."

"Do I have a boyfriend?" I ask uncertainly. Because if I do, I certainly don't remember it.

Gavin looks unsettled and ignores my question.

"You know," he muses. "I could have totally played this whole situation to my advantage. Let's start over again. Ask me again if you are a virgin."

I smile. "Am I a virgin?"

He shakes his head solemnly. "No. You're not. You and I have wild, passionate jungle sex about four times a day. You love it. And we should probably take it back up again. I think it would help your recovery process to get back into your normal routine."

I roll my eyes and giggle, ignoring the disapproving look of an elderly lady with a walker.

"Only four times a day?" I ask innocently. "Are we slackers, then?"

"Oh, don't tempt me," Gavin answers. "We can increase the rate. I'm up for anything. Anytime, anywhere. That's practically my motto. Always ready. I should get that tattooed somewhere. Maybe on my ass."

I roll my eyes.

"Seriously. Do I have a boyfriend? Besides you, I mean," I amend quickly. He smiles.

"No. You don't. Not anymore."

He looks rattled now, like he wishes he wouldn't have added that last part.

"What?" I ask. "Not anymore? Who was I with? We broke up?"

Gavin is definitely uncomfortable now. He looks away and puts a lot of effort into steering me around a slower walker. I stop in the middle of the path and put my hands on my hips.

"Gavin, seriously. Just tell me. My mom doesn't seem to want to talk about any of this stuff." And I had tried several times over the course of the past week. She just changed the subject and told me that I was an honor student and was a joy as a daughter, etc, etc. She laid it on so thick that I'm actually a little suspicious of all of it.

Gavin sighs.

"You did have a boyfriend, of sorts. You told me that you weren't in love with him, that you were *in lust* with him. He took your virginity and used you to get information. And then he tried to kill our best friends and the Prime Minister of Caberra."

Chapter Eight

"Holy shit," I breathe, staring at Gavin. "You aren't joking."

Gavin shakes his head, his normally cheerful demeanor suddenly very serious.

"I wish I were," he answers. "But I'm not. Vincent Dranias was your boyfriend. You trusted him. And he screwed you over. He's in jail now."

"Jail?" I whisper. My eyes are watery and I'm annoyed by that. Apparently, I'm not supposed to cry. I'm a bad ass. I wipe at my eyes impatiently.

"Jail," Gavin confirms. "He's eighteen, so he is being tried as an adult. The whole thing isn't over...these court cases usually go on forever. But he's in jail for the duration and I can guess that he will be there forever. You can't try to assassinate the prime minister and not pay the consequences."

"And I brought that guy into our lives? So it was my fault?"

I am horrified at this notion, even though I don't remember Dante or his father or our lives right now. Gavin shakes his head.

"No. You didn't bring him into our lives. Another one of our friends, Nate Gerraris, did. His father used to be Dante's father's Deputy Prime Minister. It was all a plot by Nate to try and get his father promoted to Dimitri's job. You were collateral damage. They used you to get close to Dante." He stares at me. "Are you okay?"

I'm not sure.

"Does Dante hate me?" I whisper. I don't remember Dante, but I certainly don't want one of my good friends to hate me. And my freaking emotions are going to be the death of me today. Only a lunatic would be paranoid that a friend that she can't even remember hates her. I'm not in love with myself right now. That much is true.

Gavin grabs my arm and guides me to a bench nearby.

"Of course he doesn't hate you," he says firmly as we sit. The wood is hard beneath my thighs, but I welcome it. It's a nice distraction from the confused mess that my brain has become.

"I know you don't remember him right now. Or me, either," Gavin continues. "But I know that you will. One of these days. And until then, just take my word for it when I say that we are your real friends. We have been friends since we were toddlers. No one understands us like we understand each other. Dante would never be mad at you for getting taken advantage of. He was more pissed than anyone that you were used."

Gavin is fierce now and it seems out of his character. I tug on his arm to get his attention.

"Calm down," I tell him. "It's okay. I believe you."

His face relaxes and he smiles down at me.

"Sorry," he says. "I get worked up sometimes."

"I can see that," I answer. "But that's good. It means you're passionate."

"Oh, baby, you have no idea," he replies, cocky once again. I pick up his hand and study it, noting his smooth fingers. He doesn't do manual labor, that much is apparent.

"You don't stay serious for long, do you?" I ask, glancing back up at his face.

His eyes are serious now, even though he grins. "What is the point in that?" he answers. "There is enough serious shit in the world. I don't need to be a party to it. We see it around us all of the time. There is no need to take ourselves seriously, too."

And in this moment, I see something in Gavin that I wonder if I ever saw before, pre-head-injury.

He's not as cocky or as happy-go-lucky on the inside as he pretends to be. He wants to be, but he isn't. So he chooses to act like it instead.

Interesting.

"Do we have hard lives?" I ask, instead of pointing out my new revelation. Gavin laughs.

"Seriously? Our fathers are both in the parliamentary cabinet of the prime minister. We want for nothing."

"That's not what I asked," I point out. "Our lives… are they hard?"

Gavin stares at me for just a moment before he shrugs, then looks away.

"It isn't always easy. But we make it work. We've been brought up this way and it is what we know."

His answer is very telling, as is the very diplomatic way he delivers it.

We're the children of politicians. It's can't be fun but Gavin is so stoic about it, so matter of fact. It's impressive. So I tell him that.

He shakes his head and helps me to my feet.

"It's not impressive," he tells me. "It's just the way it is, Mi. You're the same way. Well, you used to be. Although, you're more of a rebel than I am."

"So, I'm a bad ass rebel now?" I tease. He nods.

"You always have been. Your latest thing was hilarious."

We step back into the hospital and immediately I breathe in the sterile air, which makes me want to gag.

"My latest thing?" I repeat as Gavin punches at the elevator button.

He nods. "Yep. You were into wearing black all the time and dying your hair crazy colors. You even had your nose pierced—right before your accident. It was driving your mom insane."

I subconsciously pull at a tendril of my dark hair. "My hair isn't dyed now and I don't have a nose ring."

"I know," Gavin answers as he puts a hand on the door to make sure it stays open while everyone steps on. "When I came to visit you for the first time after the accident, your hair color had been changed and the stud in your nose had been taken out. You weren't even awake yet."

I stare at him. So that meant that my parents had dyed my hair while I was still in a coma? What the eff? Changing my hair color was a priority for them while the state of my health was still in the air?

Gavin sees my expression and shrugs.

"Political family," he reminds me.

I think it's possible that I'm going to hate my new life.

And my old life.

As we get off on my floor, Gavin turns to me.

"Mia, everything is what we make it. You hated all of the pressure placed on you by your father's job. You railed against it all of the time- but that only put more stress on you than necessary. The hole in your nose has grown closed because it was such a new piercing. It's like it never happened. So, why not use that to your advantage? If you just go with the flow like I do, everything is so much easier. You don't need stress right now. You need to relax so that your brain can recover from your injury. Seriously."

I stare at him. "Are you telling me to fall into the whole rank and file thing and do what everyone tells me?"

He grimaces.

"It sounds bad when you put it that way." He pulls me to the side, out of the way of the scurrying nurses and orderlies. "All I'm saying is... relax and go with the flow. I want you to get better and your doctor says that you need to relax to do it. My phone number is in your phone. Call me whenever you need to."

My phone. I had forgotten that I had one. And my mother certainly hadn't given it to me over the course of the last week. I wonder if it was destroyed in the earthquake?

But instead of saying anything, I just nod.

"Okay. Thank you, Gavin. I feel more normal today than I have since I woke up and I know that it is because of you. Thank you."

Gavin smiles beatifically and my knees momentarily weaken. He truly is gorgeous. He leans forward and kisses my cheek.

"Anything for you, Mi," he says. "Seriously."

And then he's gone. I'm standing in the middle of the hall by myself, watching his cocky back retreat to the elevators. Yes, even his back is cocky. And strong. I gulp.

He turns before he gets on the elevator and grins one last time. I gulp again before I smile back.

After the elevator doors swallow him up, I truly do feel alone. He knew me. The real me. Not the me that my mother is trying to make me believe that I am. Suddenly, all I want is for him to come back, to sit by my bed and hold my hand and make everything okay.

But that's impossible, because everything isn't okay.

So with a sigh, I return to my room and find my mother doing a crossword puzzle in her chair. When I enter, she smiles.

"How was your walk, sweetheart?" she asks. "Are you tired now? Would you like to lie down?"

I shake my head. "No, I feel good. The fresh air was nice and it was good to talk with Gavin. Mom, do you have my phone?"

She freezes for a second and I don't know why. But then she relaxes.

"Of course, sweetie. I've kept it in my purse. I didn't know if you'd be up to looking at your old pictures or whatnot."

She's acting strange, but I put it out of my mind. Who am I to say if she's acting strange? I don't remember her prior to this week.

She hands me my phone. It's in a hot pink case with a black and white skull on the back. The skull has a pink bow on its head. That makes me smile.

I power it on, but then am startled by a password screen.

I don't remember the password, because I don't remember anything. I look at my mom and she's already shaking her head.

"I don't know it, sweetheart. You were always very protective of it. You're a pretty private person."

Eff.

I am utterly dejected. Until I remember something. Gavin knows everything about me. Maybe he would know this. So I ask my mother for his number and I use her phone to call him.

"Hello?" he answers.

"Gav," I reply. "Do you know the password to my cell phone?"

There is a pause.

"Not for sure," he finally says. "But you usually use your birthdate for everything. I think it's your debit card pin number and your combination to your locker at school. So you might want to try that."

"Great," I mutter. "That would be helpful if I knew my birthday."

I sigh and Gavin chuckles.

"It's May 17th, so try 1705," he tells me. "And you're seventeen years old."

I roll my eyes. "I already knew that part."

Because they'd already told me.

"How much do you actually know about me?" I ask him. I can't help but smile. It really does feel good to know that at least someone remembers important things about my life. He laughs.

"I pretty much know everything," he confirms. "And if I don't know it, then Reece does."

Reece. The best friend that I can't remember.

I sigh again, trying to place her face in my head, but failing. I thank Gavin and hang up, picking up my phone once again. I punch in my birthday and Gavin was right. It opens right up.

A picture of me and a blonde girl stares back at me from my screensaver. Her slender arm is wrapped around my shoulders. My hair is two shades darker than it is right now and there are bright pink stripes threaded through it. The blonde girl is gorgeous with white blonde high-lights and sparkling blue eyes. We're both holding up the "rock on" signal with our hands and grinning into the camera. I don't know who took the picture and in fact, I don't remember taking the picture at all.

Because this is the story of my life now.

I'm perpetually clueless.

I turn the phone towards my mom.

"Is this Reece?"

My mother almost flinches before she nods.

"You don't like Reece?" I ask curiously. My mother shakes her head.

"It's not that. Reece is a charming girl. I just don't think that she understands what it's like to be you. I worry about the influence she has on you. You should be around kids who understand."

I am confused.

"Kids who understand what?"

"Kids who understand what it is like to be you," she says firmly but still vaguely. "An important member of Caberran society."

My mom sure does think a lot of herself and our family. Important members of society? I sigh.

"So it's not okay to have friends that aren't from here?"

My mother practically grits her teeth.

"That's not what I said, Mia. I just said that I prefer it when you hang around with kids who understand you. Like Dante or Gavin."

"Dante's not here," I remind her. "Are you saying that you only want me to hang around with Gavin?"

It's my mother's turn to sigh.

"No. Stop putting words in my mouth. I'd like it if you hung around with Elena Kontou, also, but you don't seem to want to. I don't know why. She's a lovely girl who knows what it's like to be a girl in your position. Plus, you really should mend fences with her."

I stare at her. "Mend fences?"

"Vincent Dranias, that boy who you snuck around with and dated, is the reason her face was scarred. You've never apologized for that."

I suck in a breath.

"Gavin told me that it wasn't my fault. That Vincent completely deceived me. Why then, would I need to apologize? I'm honestly asking—because I don't remember anything. And was she badly hurt in that explosion?"

My mother pats my hand.

"No, it wasn't your fault. But Elena seems to think that you brought that boy into everyone's lives. You really should take the time to explain that you didn't. That you were deceived along with everyone else. And no, she wasn't seriously injured, but her cheek was scarred. And she is a beautiful girl. She's taking it hard. In fact, I believe she's here in the hospital right now. She's undergoing a series of surgeries to repair the scar."

I am quiet. "I would like to talk to her and to apologize for any hand that I had in the whole mess. But the problem is, I don't remember any of it. How can I apologize for something that I don't remember?"

My mom offers me a little smile. A tight, tight smile.

"I don't know, Mia," she sighs. "But maybe you should try talking to her and just see what happens. We can get her room number from the nurse."

I nod and she leaves the room, presumably to talk with the nurse. I continue looking through my phone. I have hundreds of pictures. Reece and I are in many of them. We're on a boat, we're by the beach, we're in a bedroom. In one, we're dressed in green matching shirts, presumably from work. Gavin told me that I work for Dante's father. It looks like we are great friends.

There are pictures of Gavin. There are pictures of Gavin and I together. And there are pictures of us with another boy. A really, really handsome blonde boy who has to be Dante.

Dante Giliberti.

I look at the handsome face smiling at me from my phone and I wonder how I could possibly not remember him. He's movie star handsome. I should remember him. But I don't.

I scroll through the other faces in the pictures and I don't remember any of them, either. Charming Reece Ellis. Cocky Gavin Ariastasis. Gorgeous Dante Giliberti. I should know them. I should have their faces memorized.

But I don't.

And it is oh-so-frustrating.

I am practically growling when my mom returns.

"Room 402," she tells me. "Elena's on the fourth floor. She's here only for today and then she'll be gone. So you should go see her now while you have the chance."

I am hesitant, but my mom is insistent.

"Mia," she says patiently. "You have known Elena since you were children. You shouldn't let a misunderstanding like this ruin things. Just go and speak with her. I'm sure you'll be pleasantly surprised."

I am still unsure, but I go anyway. How can I not? I have to make sense out of my life somehow. I should begin by piecing it back together.

I creep out into the hall and take a big mouthful of the medicinal hospital smell. It smells like iodine and alcohol and plastic. I hate it. But I timidly make my way through the bustling corridors and sterile halls until I find myself standing in front of room 402.

I stand there for a few minutes, trying to get my courage up.

You can do this.

You can do this.

You can effing do this.

My hand shakes and I silently cuss myself out. *Listen, you. I don't know who you used to be. But I know that you are not such a wuss. You are a badass. Buck the eff up.*

I knock lightly and there is no answer. I knock harder.

"Come in," an annoyed voice calls. I swallow hard and stick my shoulders back. I don't know who I used to be, but I don't like feeling intimidated by anyone now. My chin juts out and I push the door open.

A beautiful girl lies in the bed, covered up to her waist by blankets. She's got hair the deepest shade of red that flows in soft waves over her shoulders. Her eyes are emerald green and narrowed as she looks at me. And there is a bandage on her cheekbone, marring what would otherwise be a perfect face. She's breathtakingly beautiful. And she looks like she hates me.

I gulp.

"Elena?" I ask, although I'm sure it is. Who else could it be?

"Yes," she answers coolly in a voice that borders on hatred. "Were you expecting someone else?"

I shake my head. "No. I just wanted to sure."

Elena smiles a frigid smile that reminds me slightly of a piranha. I don't know why because her smile is gorgeous and perfect.

And cold.

Just like the rest of her.

"Ah, yes. I forgot. You can't remember anything."

She doesn't look disturbed by that at all. She seems ambivalent, actually.

Even though she hasn't invited me, I walk inside and sit in the chair next to her bed. She has fashion magazines everywhere, so I move them to clear a space.

"My mother told me that you and I have a misunderstanding and that I should clear it up," I tell her. "But I don't remember anything. So it's hard to know what to say."

Elena studies me with interest. "You truly don't remember anything at all?" she asks. "Not a thing?"

I shake my head. "Not much at all. I remember my car. And I don't know why. I remember scuba diving. But I don't remember my friends. I don't remember my parents and I don't remember myself."

"So you don't remember me?" Elena asks, her lovely head cocked. I shake my head again. "You don't remember growing up with me?"

"No. I'm sorry. I don't."

And she laughs. I am startled by this and stare. It definitely wasn't the reaction that I was expecting.

She muffles her giggles and then stares back.

"I'm sorry," she says. "It's not funny. It's ironic."

"How is it ironic?" I ask suspiciously. I don't know what to make of this girl.

Elena giggles again. I'm not sure if she's laughing at me or with me or what.

"You've always worked so hard to portray an image… the image of a girl who doesn't care about who she is. And here you are now… you don't remember any of it. You truly don't know who you are. Don't you find that funny at all?"

And suddenly, I kind of do.

I laugh with her.

"If I remembered it, it would be funnier," I finally tell her. "But I don't. I saw pictures—of my hair and my clothes. I guess I was trying hard to prove a point."

Elena nods. "You definitely were trying to make a point."

I look at her and try not to look at her bandage. But it's hard. It might as well have a sign on it that says *Look at me.* My eyes keep gravitating toward it. I force them back to hers.

"I'm sorry," I tell her. "For whatever part I played in the accident. I'm told that I didn't know what was going on, that I was tricked along with everyone else. But if there were signs that I should have seen and didn't, I'm really sorry about that."

Elena's nose tilts up and I wonder if this is the moment that she's going to let me have it. She's got a certain bitchy air about her…she's definitely a girl who knows what she wants and how to get it. She doesn't mess around. I may have amnesia, but even I can see that.

And she is silent for a long, long moment. I think she's trying to make up her mind.

"I was pissed at you," she finally admits to me. And she sounds surprisingly candid. "But I was pissed at everyone, to be honest. I know that it wasn't you who did this to me. It was Nate Geraris and Vincent Dranias. It's just difficult to be mad at people who aren't here. I seem to need something- or someone- that I can focus my aggression on."

"You might want to take up target shooting instead," I tell her wryly. She laughs.

"I don't think anyone wants to see a gun in my hand," she admits. She seems more honest than I was expecting. Although I don't know why I had any expectations at all. I don't remember her.

OhmyGod. I'm so tired of that phrase. *I don't remember.* I get it already. I'm clueless about everything.

"Were we friends?" I ask curiously. "My mother said that we didn't hang out much, but that she didn't know why. But I'm guessing that my mother didn't know everything there was to know about me, either."

Elena stares at me silently. She's examining me, picking me apart. But why?

"No, we weren't very good friends," she tells me finally. "I don't know why. I guess I'm not always a nice person. And you never tolerated any crap. That intimidated me."

I'm an intimidating bad ass?

I'm not sure that I like me very much.

"So you were the mean girl and I was the bad ass?" I guess. She smiles slowly.

"I suppose so."

"My mother thinks that I should try to be friends with you," I tell her bluntly. "Because you understand what it's like to be me—a child of a political family. Do you want to be friends?"

Elena stares at me in surprise. I can tell that she doesn't know what to say. She wasn't expecting this from me. But I wasn't expecting any of this from her, either, so I guess we're even.

"Well, you're certainly not any less blunt," she observes. "You've always said exactly what was on your mind. Okay, Mia. We can try to be friends. It should be interesting."

"Yes," I answer quietly. "It should be interesting."

We chat for a little while longer and it seems uncomfortable, but it gets easier toward the end. I finally make my way toward the door and close it behind me. I exhale a long breath and lean against it.

Why do I feel like I just made a deal with the devil?

That's ridiculous. Right?

Elena might have red hair, but she's not the devil.

I spend the rest of the walk to my own room trying to convince myself of that.

Chapter Nine

I press my face against the glass of my mother's car. I leave a nose print, but I don't care. The hills of Caberra speed past us as my mom winds through the curvy roads toward Giliberti House.

Apparently, our house is uninhabitable and will have to be re-built in order for us to return home. Until then, my mother and I will be staying at Dimitri Giliberti's family home, Giliberti House. It is located in a huge estate surrounded by olive groves outside of Valese.

Also apparently, I've been there a million times before because that is where I work...in their gift shop. I sell gourmet olive oils and whatnot. And I say 'whatnot' because I have no idea what else I sell there. Sigh.

"We're almost there," my mom says. I know she's assuming that my sigh was a result of being in the car. "You'll see the olive groves soon."

And I do. We round one more curve and I see hundreds of olive trees, their lush green tops touching the sky. The olives look like pebbles on the branches.

"Your father will come out on the weekends," my mother tells me. "He's going to stay in the city during the week for work reasons. He's worried about you, though. He's hoping that the peace and quiet out here will help you relax and recover more quickly."

Him and me both.

I'm sick of this whole can't-remember-who-I-am-thing.

I nod wordlessly, taking in the scenery as my mother turns into a long, long drive. Flowering trees line each side and white blossoms drift through the air, padding the stone lane beneath us with a thick blanket of petals. It looks like a painting. I take a whiff of the sweet-smelling air.

"It's gorgeous here, right?" my mother asks, lifting an eyebrow.

"Yes," I agree. "It is."

She pulls into a circular drive and we get out of the car. The house is amazingly beautiful, like something out of a fancy fairytale. Warm light floods from the windows onto the manicured lawn around it. It draws me to it and makes me want to run into the house.

A tiny little woman comes out, stooped and elderly. But she moves quickly. She is down the stairs before I can even speak. Her hair is pulled into a neat chignon at the nape of her neck.

"Mia!" she cries out and barrels into me, grasping me up into a surprisingly strong bear hug. She smells like cookies. And maybe sunshine.

I look at her blankly, wish-wish-wishing that I could place her. Because she clearly knows me. She looks at me sympathetically.

"I'm sorry, sweet girl," she tells me, taking a step backward. "I forgot that you don't remember me. My name is Marionette Papou. I run this household for the Gilibertis. You know me very well, little one. I've known you since you were in pigtails. But you will remember. I have faith in that."

She is confident. I like that.

She turns and greets my mother and then her husband, Darius, introduces himself to me before he gets our bags. They both move surprisingly quickly for being older. And I am surprised again when Marionette tells me that Darius is the foreman for the olive groves. They have both worked here for decades, apparently, and they have no intentions of slowing down anytime soon.

They lead us into the massive house and I immediately feel welcomed, like I am home. The house is immaculately furnished, but it is cozy even as it is magnificent and enormous. It is the kind of place where families live and thrive. I feel instantly at ease.

Marionette smiles.

"I have a treat for you," she tells me with a grin. "Your favorite."

I have no idea what my favorite is, but I follow her anyway.

I'm trusting that way, I guess.

As Darius takes our bags upstairs to our rooms, Marionette leads us to the kitchen. Wonderful smells surround us and I inhale deeply.

She hands me a saucer and shoves me into a chair.

"Your favorite," she tells me again as I look at the little fancy plate. There is a forest green G inscribed on the china rim. A flaky croissant drizzled in butter instantly makes my mouth water. "I make them from scratch," she adds proudly.

I take a bite and instantly am in love with Marionette. I tell her that and she laughs.

"Oh, you fell in love with me long ago, little one," she grins, before she pats my arm and glides away to wipe off a cabinet. "I'm French. Everyone loves me."

I don't know what that has to do with anything, but it makes me smile anyway. I consider that as I look around. This kitchen reminds me of a giant farm kitchen, but is filled with every modern convenience. It's comfortable in here. I could stay in here forever.

My mother, however, must feel differently.

"Mia, I'm going to go unpack," she tells me. "If you need me, Marionette will show you to my room."

I nod and watch her walk away. She doesn't seem very happy to be here. But then again, she doesn't seem all that happy to be anywhere. I wonder why. And then I wonder if I *ever* knew why.

Marionette watches me.

"Your mother worries about you," she says quietly. "I know you don't believe that, but it is true."

I am startled. "I don't believe that?" I ask curiously. "Do my mom and I have issues?"

It's Marionette's turn to look startled, like a cat who swallowed a canary.

"Uh. Not necessarily," she says slowly. "Just typical teenager and mother things. Nothing big."

But she turns and focuses very hard on cleaning the already spotless stone counters. I narrow my eyes suspiciously, but I don't say anything. Clearly, she doesn't want to say anything else.

"Is it alright if I go for a walk outside?" I ask her politely. She turns and smiles.

"Little girl, you don't have to ask permission. This is your home, for as long as you need it to be. Feel free to walk anywhere you would like to walk."

I smile and impulsively turn and hug her. She's the warmest person that I've met so far. She seems surprised, but she hugs me back tightly. Her tiny arms are surprisingly strong.

"It's good to have you here," she tells me and I swear that her faded eyes are wet. But she turns away again before I can tell for sure.

I make my way outside through the back terrace doors.

I look around and sigh contentedly. If there was ever a nirvana, this is it. Giliberti House is like an oasis in the middle of the country. Rolling hills surround us, swaying trees encircle us and the smell of fresh flowers assails my senses. It's an enchanting place.

And then I hear it.

Whistling.

A song with no words and no real melody.

I perk my ears and try to find where it is coming from.

I walk past the back gardens and over the shady lane leading down to what looks to be a set of barns. And then I see him.

Sweet. Mother. Of Mary.

A muscular guy with sandy blonde hair is shirtless and there are so many muscles rippling that I can't even count them all. He is working with a gigantic horse and he is whistling.

And I am panting.

Holy crap.

Do I know this guy??

I am frozen as I watch his biceps flex and move. He looks to be about my age. He's got broad shoulders, slim hips and he's really tall. He's wearing cowboy boots.

Cowboy boots.

Who is he??

My curiosity is firmly piqued, so I decide to just find out. I approach him and after a second, he notices me and stops what he is doing.

And then he grins a grin so devastating, I think it might stop my heart.

No. Lie.

"Mia!" he calls.

Holy crap. I do know him. Or he knows me, anyway. I watch as he grabs a cowboy hat that is hanging on a fence post and slaps it on his head as he hops over the fence to the paddock. He reaches me in literally five long strides and then crunches me in a bear hug.

I want to die right here, I think.

In the safety of his strong arms.

I will stay here for the next sixty years and die a happy woman.

But obviously, after a second, he steps away and I fight the urge to cling to him. He feels so safe and warm. And clearly I am craving security. I might want to see a therapist about that.

"You look great!" he tells me with a grin. "Your stripes are gone, though."

I automatically run my fingers through my hair. "I know. I don't... I don't remember them."

Hot Guy looks pensive.

"I bet you don't remember me, either, do you?" he asks softly. I am hesitant, because I really, really wish that I did. But I don't. So I shake my head.

"I'm sorry," I tell him. "Maybe soon. They keep telling me that my memories should come back soon. I'm starting to hate that word, actually. *Soon*. It's so vague."

Hot Guy holds his hand out.

"My name is Quinn McKeyen," he tells me as he shakes my hand formally. "I'm living here at Giliberti House for the school year. I'm in the Foreign Exchange Student program. I'm from Kansas- which is the state in America where your friend Reece is from. Do you remember Reece?"

I shake my head again. "I don't remember anything at all," I admit.

He actually smiles. "I'm going to have to think of some way to use that to my advantage," he says with a wink. I shake my head.

"Don't even try it," I laugh. "Gavin already tried, but unfortunately for him, he didn't think about it fast enough. He told me about the state of my love life before-hand. That was a little counter-productive."

Quinn laughs again. And I decide that I might not know him, but I freaking love his laugh. And his American accent.

"Are you a cowboy?" I ask him, eyeing the way that sweat is rolling off his abdomen. I fight the urge to lick it.

Gross. Lick sweat? What is wrong with me?

Am I a freak?

He smiles. "Yes, I guess you could say that. I like to ride things. Does that make you nervous?"

I stare him blankly. "Nervous? Why would I be...oh." His meaning hits me like a truck and I blush. "I get it. You like to ride things."

I smile, even though I'm pretty sure my mom would kill me for engaging in this conversation. But what she doesn't know won't hurt her, right?

"And, no," I add. "I'm not nervous. I can handle anything."

"But you don't even know who you are," Quinn reminds me with another grin. "So how can you handle *anything*?"

I love the fact that he doesn't pussy-foot around me. Everyone else has been and it has grown so annoying. I don't need to be handled with kid gloves. I'm not going to break.

"True," I concede. "What all do you ride, beside women and horses?"

Quinn's dark eyes sparkle. And I find myself transfixed by that. His eyes are such a dark brown, like a rich gourmet chocolate. I'm mesmerized by them.

"I ride four-wheelers, horses, bulls, you name it. But I haven't seen any bulls in Caberra yet, so I've settled for Titan. Dante bought him for Reece when they were still here. She told me that I can mess with him."

He gestures toward the enormous devil of a horse behind him. I eye the beast cautiously.

"Titan looks a little dangerous," I point out. Quinn only grins. He's so relaxed in his worn-out jeans and boots. He's like the epitome of country charm. I gulp.

"Oh, I sort of like a little danger from time to time," he tells me. "It keeps things interesting."

"Oh, really?" I shake my head. "It's all fun and games until you wind up in the hospital."

Quinn laughs. "I'm very good at handling danger, so don't worry. Everything will be fine."

"Will it?" I ask and Quinn nods.

"Yes."

And I don't even know what we're talking about anymore. I've been distracted by his handsome good looks and his charm and all of the sexual innuendoes that have been flying around.

"Do you want a ride?" Quinn asks. I'm startled because I've been staring so hard into his eyes that I wasn't expecting him to speak.

"On Titan?" I stutter.

He laughs.

"Unless you have a better idea," he says with one brow raised. He patiently waits for my answer while I die of embarrassment. I can literally feel the heat splashing across my cheeks.

"Uh, no. I don't have a better idea," I stammer. I don't know where my wits have all gone. They seem to be missing in action. I curse them silently and order them to come back. They silently laugh at me and then run for the hills. I have rogue wits.

Quinn's damned eyes continue to sparkle.

"Well, that's a pity. If you think of something, let me know. Until then, yes, I was speaking of the horse."

"I don't know how to ride," I tell him. "At least, I don't think I do. Do I?"

Quinn shakes his head. "I don't know. You and I just met awhile back. Horses aren't all that common here in Caberra, though. So I doubt it. But I heard that you'll be staying here for a while. Maybe I could teach you. We could work out a trade. You teach me to swim, I'll teach you to ride."

I stare at him hesitantly. "I don't know if I remember how to swim. But if I do, I'll be happy to teach you."

Quinn throws his head back and laughs.

"Mia, you are a constant surprise. I never know what to think with you. I like it. Okay, it's a deal. If you remember how to swim, you can teach me. And I'll teach you to ride regardless. Deal?"

I nod immediately, because the image of me sitting in front of him on that horse, leaned back against his strong chest between his legs, is enough to give me heart palpations.

For real.

"Deal," I agree.

"Now, how about I lead you around for a bit on Titan. I'll have a hold of his head the whole time so there is nothing to be afraid of," Quinn tells me. My chin automatically juts out on its own accord.

"I'm not afraid of anything," I announce. And then I'm startled by that. I'm not? Those words came out on their own. I didn't even think about them. It was Old Mia talking. Maybe I like her, after all.

Quinn appraises me and there is appreciation in his eyes.

"Come on, then," he tells me, holding his large hand out. I take it and he leads me into the paddock. He holds his hand out to Titan, who huffs a big breath out of his gigantic flared nostrils before he steps closer to Quinn.

Quinn snaps a lead rope into the ring on the halter and I fight the urge to run. What was I thinking, agreeing to this? Titan is enormous. And he's looking at me with the wild eyes of a demon as he stomps the dirt with his huge demon hoof.

Ohmygod.

I'm an idiot.

This horse is a freaking demon.

Quinn looks at my face and laughs.

"Come on, Miss I'm-Not-Scared. It's alright."

He makes a cup out of his hands and motions for me to use it. I wedge my foot between his fingers and he boosts me up. I swing my other leg around and before I know it, I'm situated on top of the demon.

HolyHell.

I'm an idiot with amnesia who is sitting on a demon.

A very tall demon.

I gulp.

"Calm down," Quinn tells me as he glances up at me. "Horses can sense fear. There's nothing to be afraid of. I've got you." He pats my leg before he walks to Titan's head. And I can feel the imprint of where his hand was on my thigh. I swallow. He has a very sexy hand. Both hands, actually.

"You know, in America, horses are sometimes used for therapy," Quinn tells me conversationally, as he leads Titan out of the coral. I am panicky as we leave the confines of the fence. A fence means safety. And since I am outside of that fence, I am no longer safe. I swallow hard.

"Are you saying that I need therapy now?" I ask, only half joking. I clench my thighs around Titan's bare, broad back. I so don't want to fall off. There's no way that Quinn could catch me in time and I'd break my neck. I fight the urge to leap off and run for the house.

Quinn glances back up at me.

"Oh, you've probably always needed it," he tells me. "I've never met anyone who tried so hard to be someone that she's not."

That definitely gives me pause.

It's almost the same exact thing that Elena said.

"I'm kidding," he chuckles as he sees my expression. "You did try hard to portray a certain image. But I'm sure you didn't need therapy. Just a reality check."

I stare at him.

"A reality check? How well did you know me, anyway?"

Quinn shakes his head and wipes a little sweat from his brow. He's got a strong jawline. I love that. I fight to focus on his words, not his face. It's a difficult feat to master.

"Not that well. But you were fairly easy to read. Not so much now, though."

That pacifies me a little.

Sort of.

"Why not now?" I ask slowly.

Quinn looks at me uncertainly. "Because it's hard to read someone who doesn't know who she is."

"Who do you think I am?" I am practically whispering now. I suddenly feel very, very tired. I'm physically tired, I'm mentally tired and losing my identity is just a bit exhausting.

Quinn stops and turns to me, taking a step and then another, until he is pressed against my leg and staring into my eyes.

"I think you're a sweet little bird who has always tried to break out of her cage because you really had no idea what life is like outside of your world. And now you're a sweet little bird who doesn't know what to think. All of your masks are gone and now you are forced to be yourself. It must be scary for you."

He doesn't sound sympathetic, just matter-of-fact.

And I have to respect that.

I nod.

"I'm not a bird," I tell him. "But you're right about one thing. I don't have anything to hide behind now, that's for sure."

"Why would you want to hide at all?" Quinn asks, still staring into my eyes. "That's the part I could never figure out. You don't have anything to hide from. You can take life by the tail if you want to. It's yours for the taking."

"What's mine for the taking?" I ask, momentarily confused by his nearness. He smiles.

"Anything you want."

I suck in my breath.

And he inhales deeply.

And then the moment is broken by my mother's shrill screaming.

"Mia Alexandria Giannis. Get off of that animal! You're going to break your neck!" I turn and find her rushing out of Giliberti House toward us and Quinn grins at me.

"I take it back. You might want to hide from *that*."

I smile back as warmth floods through me. He lifts me down and I enjoy the feeling of my body pressed against his, even though it only lasts for a second. His heart beats against mine.

Ba-bump.

Ba-bump.

He glances down at me and his eyes are like melted chocolate. And I want to eat him up.

Eat him up?

Yep. With a freaking spoon.

I'm insane.

But he makes me feel so good.

That's a fact that I come to realize as I turn away from him to meet my mother. Quinn walks away to take Titan back to the stables and I miss him immediately. Just like I missed Gavin in the hospital yesterday.

They both make me feel good in two different ways.

I sigh.

Because I know that I'm in trouble. I don't even know who I am, but I just woke up from a coma and I find that I want two separate boys for two separate reasons. That can never be good.

At least I know that much.

Chapter Ten

Dinner at Giliberti House is interesting.

Marionnette, Darius and Quinn eat in the kitchen, because that's the way they've been doing it. Quinn apparently didn't want to eat in the formal dining room alone and the Papous would never eat in there because they don't consider that proper behavior. They are staff, after all. Even though they seem more like family.

But my mother refuses to eat in the kitchen.

"Mia," she sighs. "The wife and daughter of Stanyos Giannis cannot eat in the kitchen. It just isn't seemly."

So, we eat in the formal dining room.

Alone.

And it feels so stuffy and unnatural. And I hate it.

As I stare down the long table at my mother, I hate it even more. I have to practically yell so that she can hear me. That's how big this table is.

I want to join the others in the kitchen, where it is warm and cozy and because Quinn is there. But that's not going to happen. My mother told me as much. Right after she threatened my life if I ever got on a horse again. And told me that I need to stay away from Quinn. Which of course, for some reason, had the immediate and opposite effect. I want to be near him more than ever.

Apparently, I'm rebellious.

So, I do what any rebellious girl would probably do.

I eat in sullen silence. I drink my soup from the spoon, I eat three croissants (because they really are my favorites) and I have a giant piece of pie.

My mother looks at me in disapproval.

"Mia, you're not going to be seventeen forever. You might want to start watching what you eat. You don't want to gain weight."

I roll my eyes. I've got plenty of other things to worry about besides my weight. I'm skinny for now and that's all that matters. I'll worry about my weight when I'm thirty.

"How long is the construction on our house going to take?" I yell down to my mom. She cringes from the volume of my voice. I'm guessing that it isn't seemly. But how else is she supposed to hear me? This table is five miles long.

And I'm seriously starting to hate the word *seemly.*

She shrugs. "They say it will take three months or so. And Kolettis Academy will be closed for the next two to four weeks for construction, as well. I just heard today. They will add that time onto the end of the year. So don't worry. You'll graduate on time."

I nod. I'm happy about being out of school for a month. Hopefully that will give my memory time to come back. I'll focus on that.

"My doctor said that I should do things that are familiar to me," I remind her. "He said that it will help my memory. I think I'll see if Gavin wants to go scuba diving tomorrow."

My mother looks pained, but she nods. I'm betting that she would much rather have me spend time with Gavin, even if we're doing something she hates, rather than spend time with Quinn. I don't know why and I don't really care. I guess that's Old Mia's spunk talking.

I'm sort of digging that chick now and I wish I could remember more about her.

"Also, Marionette told me that Dante and Reece are returning to Caberra for a while to help with clean-up from the earthquake," my mother tells me. "The downtown area was particularly damaged. It might do you good to help, as well."

"Dante and Reece are coming?" I ask, surprised. "When?"

She shakes her head. "I don't know. Marionette probably does, though. You can ask her."

I'm excited by this. Dante and Reece used to be familiar to me. If I talk with them, it might help. This is a good thing.

I immediately pick up my dinner plate and head to the kitchen, ignoring my mother's protests. She doesn't follow. Too unseemly, I guess, to follow your daughter into a kitchen. I almost laugh, but don't. My mother's self-imposed rules are sort of funny. And sort of pathetic.

Marionette, Darius and Quinn look surprised to see me, but Quinn quickly jumps up and pulls a chair out for me. His polite behavior makes my pulse speed up. But I try to calm it down. He's only exhibiting manners. Geez. I'm sure he'd do it for anyone.

I sit down and immediately turn to Marionette, asking her about Dante and Reece. Her face is genuinely happy when she answers.

"They'll be here soon," she tells me. "I think they're arriving tomorrow. And they are very excited to see you."

Quinn doesn't look quite as happy, but I'm guessing that has something to do with the fact that he and Reece have a complicated relationship or so I'm told.

Apparently, they took turns having a crush on each other for the last ten years or so. But they never timed it right and so they never ended up together.

Quinn dated Reece's friend Becca for the last couple of years, although now they're broken up. But now Reece is with Dante, so the timing still isn't right. I wonder if Quinn is regretful of that?

He doesn't seem to be, though, as he takes a bite of soup. I can't help but notice how big his hands are. He's absolutely gigantic.

"So, how much trouble did you get into for riding Titan?" he asks, grinning. He isn't apologetic at all. I like it.

"Not much," I answer. "Just a lecture. Apparently, I'm supposed to stay away from you, too. But you can see how well that lecture took."

Marionette mutters under her breath and I can see that she doesn't approve of my mother. That's okay. I'm not sure that I do, either. Quinn's eyes sparkle.

"Am I a bad influence?" he asks with interest. "I think I might like that. I've never been the bad boy before. It might be fun."

"You've never been the bad boy?" I ask doubtfully. My eyebrows are raised. Quinn shakes his head.

"Nope. I'm a Midwesterner, remember? Oh, I guess you don't. Well, I'm from the heartland of America where we're polite and friendly and never know a stranger. Yes, m'am. No, m'am and all that. Although I *am* considering a tattoo. I'm guessing your mom wouldn't approve of that, either."

He's smiling now, totally unrepentant and unconcerned. My pulse speeds up yet again. It seems to do that a lot around him.

"A tattoo? Gavin said that he's going to get one that says, "Always ready."

Quinn rolls his eyes good-naturedly. "He would. I haven't decided yet what I want. Maybe you can help me."

I raise my eyebrow again. "Me? I don't know you well enough to know what you should get."

Quinn winks. "Well, maybe that's part of my diabolical plan. You'll have to get to know me."

"Devious," I grin. "I like it. Well, it might backfire on you. Maybe I'll get a matching tattoo and then you'll be tied to me for life."

"Needy," he observes. "I like it."

We laugh and Marionette and Darius laugh, too. I really like them. And I like this kitchen. And I have decided that I'm going to eat in here from now on. My mother can suck it. If she doesn't want to join us, she can eat out there alone. She can keep up her seemly appearances all on her own.

When we're finished eating, Quinn walks me out. We pass through the dining room and I see that my mother is gone. She left her dirty dishes, though. Obviously carrying them to the kitchen would be unseemly. I'm really starting to hate that word. I should make a list of the words I'm starting to hate.

Seemly.

Soon.

Apparently.

I can add more later. Right now, I'm preoccupied with Quinn. And his bulging biceps, long fingers and mischievous grin. I stare up at him and smile.

"Do you and Reece get along okay now?" I ask him as we turn onto the staircase leading to the bedrooms. He looks surprised.

"Of course. Why do you ask?"

"Gavin told me about you and Reece's history. So I just wondered," I shrug. I'm trying to act nonchalant. I hope it's coming across that way. In an effort to enhance the act, I make a point of examining the portraits of Giliberti ancestors as we walk past them. Their eyes seem to stare into my back. It's sort of creepy.

"Why are you so interested?" Quinn raises an eyebrow.

So, I fail.

Epically.

Apparently I wasn't so nonchalant.

"I don't know," I shrug again. "Just curious. I guess I find everything interesting nowadays. Everything seems new."

Quinn smiles, a real and sincere smile. It's salt of the earth. Whatever that means.

"I guess that's one benefit to amnesia," he tells me, as he lightly guides my elbow around the landing. "You get to start over. If you want," he adds.

I look at him. "Should I? Start over, I mean. Was the old me something I should re-do?"

He stops.

And cocks his head.

And he is oh-so-sexy.

"No," he says firmly. "Old Mia was someone who hated the pressure of worrying about what everyone thought. So you hid who you really were. Maybe the new you won't be so concerned with it."

I stare at him.

"I thought you didn't know me that well," I point out uncertainly. He shrugs.

"It wasn't difficult to see," he answers as we resume the climb on the stairs. "Just worry about being who you really are. If you never remember who you were, that's fine. You're still you regardless."

"That's very profound," I murmur.

And it is. I've been so preoccupied with trying to remember who I was, that I forgot that I'm still me either way. I'm just a me without memories. Interesting. It's so simple that it's genius.

We stop in front of my bedroom.

There is an awkward pause. But maybe it's only awkward to me. Quinn always seems casual. Always relaxed.

He smiles at me now.

"I'm glad you're here," he tells me. "I was getting lonely here all by myself."

"Well, Dante and Reece will be here tomorrow. So, you'll have even more people to keep you company," I remind him.

"True," he acknowledges. "But I'm most happy about you."

I startle and stare into his chocolate brown eyes. "Really?" I whisper.

He nods. "Really."

"You don't hide what you're feeling much, do you?" I observe. Quinn's eyes sparkle in response.

"I don't see the point in it," he admits. "I don't like games. I don't like playing them because I hate to lose."

"So you're a sore loser , then?" I ask with a laugh.

But he's shaking his head. "Nope. I'm not a sore loser. Because I never lose in the first place."

He dips his head like an old-fashioned cowboy, like something that belongs in a razor commercial or a cologne ad. And then he continues down the hall to his bedroom and I fight the urge to chase after him.

But I don't and so I'm left standing in shock in the hallway alone.

He doesn't lose.

What is he trying to win?

I have a feeling that I am going to be the one who loses—hours of sleep tonight—trying to ponder that question.

Chapter Eleven

"Mia!"

There is a squeal, unearthly loud and shrieky, before something lands on my bed. I open my eyes but squeeze them instantly closed again. The sun is too, too bright. And the voice is too, too loud.

And too, too unfamiliar.

But the unfamiliar thing is bouncing.

And ramming its bony elbow into my side.

So I open my eyes again and find the girl from my phone.

"Reece?"

The blonde girl squeals again and hugs me. "You remember me!!"

She's exuberant and I don't want to tell her that I don't. But I kind of have to. She'd figure it out eventually anyway. So I shake my head.

"No. I'm sorry. I don't remember yet. But your pictures are in my phone."

The pretty blonde girl- Reece—is dismayed, but she quickly tries to hide it. She's like a cheerful ray of sunshine and the clouds are covering up her smile. I feel guilty about that.

"I'm really sorry," I tell her again.

"It's okay," she assures me. "You'll remember soon. I'm just so happy to see you!"

"I'm sure I would be happy to see you, too, if I could remember," I tell her regretfully. I know it's true. When I couldn't sleep last night, I went through my old text messages. I found about a million from me to Reece, demanding that she return to Caberra. Our text conversations had me laughing. She's pretty funny. I can see why I liked her.

She's shaking her head now. "Why are you still in bed? It's 9:00 a.m."

And she's looking at me almost accusingly. I narrow my eyes.

"If you try and tell me that I'm normally a morning person, I'm going to know that you're on drugs. There's no way that's true."

Reece laughs. "Heck, no. I won't even try it. I'm actually surprised that you haven't thrown a pillow at my head yet."

"Don't think I haven't thought about it," I tell her. "But since we're just meeting- for the second time- I'm trying to be on my best behavior."

She laughs again. "You're the same Mia, even if you don't remember," she tells me. "You've always had spunk. And you've still got it. That's important, I think."

"It is?" I stare at her. "I don't think my mother thinks so."

Reece smiles. "You and your mom... you've been at each other's throats since the day I met you. I doubt that's ever going to change."

"We have?" I ask with interest. "She's trying hard to make me believe that I've always been perfect... perfect manners, perfect behavior, perfect at everything. It didn't really seem in-line with what I feel."

Reece laughs now, a tinkling sound in the sunshine of my bedroom. In fact, she laughs until she is gasping for air. I find myself glaring at her.

"I don't think it was *that* funny," I tell her wryly.

"Oh, but it is," she gasps. "If you could only remember. You would just die about that."

"I must have been a monster," I mutter as I swing my legs out of bed. Reece looks at me and sobers up.

"No, of course you weren't," she tells me quickly. "You were just feisty. And you didn't take crap from anyone. And you definitely didn't try to be perfect for your mother. She has her own ideas about how the perfect family should be that you've never agreed with. You've never wanted to pretend to be someone that you're not. I've always loved that about you."

I sigh.

"It's so good to hear you say that," I admit to her. "Gavin tells me that I should just fall into rank and do what I'm told because it's easier that way. And he should know- he's in the same position as me. But it doesn't feel right. I don't want to try and change who I am just to fit an image. But apparently, that's sort of exactly what I was doing before. It seems that I was deliberately going out of my way to be the opposite of what my parents wanted me to be. I don't really want to do that either. I just want to figure out who I really am and be that."

Reece is looking at me sympathetically and I don't like that.

"Don't feel sorry for me," I tell her. "Please. I seriously hate that."

She tightens up her expression and leans over to give me a hug.

"In that case," she answers. "I'm glad to see you. Get your butt out of bed. We've got things to do and people to scare."

I laugh and she smirks.

"That's something you would have said once upon a time," she tells me. I grin.

"Well, then, let's go scare some people."

I get dressed and Reece and I go downstairs for breakfast. When we walk into the kitchen, Dante and Quinn are lounging at the table with freshly squeezed orange juice.

Together.

Which seems odd to me.

Quinn grins lazily at me and I fight the urge to dive into his lap and rub up against him like a cat. That might not go over so well, so I restrain myself.

Dante turns and his entire face lights up when he sees me.

"Mia!" he says happily.

He gets to his feet and I look him over. Yes, he's exactly as I thought he would be...like a fashion model. He's wearing khaki slacks and a button-up shirt with rolled up sleeves. The very picture of casual elegance. But he's sexy as hell with that dimple in his chin and his sparkling eyes. I smile and he hugs me.

"It's good to see you," he tells me quietly. "I've been so worried about you ever since I heard."

"It's good to see you too," I tell him. "I don't remember you right now, but I'm hoping that I will soon."

"You will," he tells me confidently. "I have faith in that. Everything will be fine."

Dante has an air of calm around him that is contagious. I feel comforted by his presence, like all will be well because he says it will be. I like that.

He pushes out the chair next to him for me and Reece sits next to Quinn. I can tell that there is no animosity there at all, they're as comfortable as old friends can be. And Dante is perfectly secure with their relationship. As he should be. It's apparent to anyone in a five mile radius that Reece is completely in love with him. Any thoughts she ever had about Quinn are long gone.

"How long are you home for?" I ask as I nibble on a fresh croissant. Dante shrugs elegantly.

"We don't really know yet," he answers. "As soon as we heard about the quake, we knew that we needed to come and help with the cleanup, especially when we heard about you. We talked my dad into it and here we are. But I don't know how long he'll let us stay."

"How can you miss school in America?" I ask curiously. Dante shrugs again.

"If we're here too long, we'll just finish out the year here. I'm not that worried about it."

I know that Old Mia would be very happy to hear this. And I'm sure that New Mia will be too. Eventually. *Soon.*

Stupid vague words.

"Reece and I have to go see my father this morning," Dante tells us. "But this afternoon, we've volunteered to help with a clean-up effort in town. Would you like to join us?"

"Of course," I say. Quinn is nodding too.

"I'd be happy to," Quinn says. He meets my gaze and my face immediately gets hot. I don't know why. I'm weird, I guess. That's a good reason. And also, I think he wants to come because I'll be there. That's a good reason, too.

OhMyWord.

That thought makes me flustered.

I'm suddenly finding it hard to breathe. I try to breathe out of my nose like a normal person, not out of my mouth like a weird mouth-breather. But panting makes that difficult.

"So, want to meet here around 2:00?" Dante asks as he stands up. "We can ride together."

"Sure," I tell him. He bends down and squeezes my shoulder.

"It really is good to see you, Mi," he tells me quietly and then gives me a peck on the cheek. I smile at him.

"It's good to see you too," I answer. And I mean it. Even if I don't remember, it is still good to see them. He and Reece are so friendly. And their blue eyes sparkle all of the time. What's not to like? They're like friendly, witty Barbie and Ken dolls. They're a gorgeous matching set.

They leave and Quinn and I are left alone at the table.

"So, what are your plans for the day?" Quinn asks. "Until 2:00, I mean?"

I shrug. "I'm not sure yet. I'm thinking about seeing if Gavin wants to go diving. I've got to see if I still know how to swim somehow. I've got a deal to uphold."

Quinn grins. "You sure do. And you don't strike me as someone who would renege."

I'm already shaking my head. "Never."

He laughs and clears his plate, putting it in the sink. I like the fact that he does that. It's a thoughtful thing, even though it's small. My gaze flickers to his butt, which is framed perfectly in worn Levi's. I seriously doubt there is a pair of jeans in the world that doesn't agree with that butt. And then he turns and catches me checking his agreeable butt out.

Epic. Fail.

I blush.

"See something you like?" he asks, one eyebrow raised.

I blush again.

"I don't know what you mean," I stammer.

He chuckles. "Wrong answer, tiny tot. You're supposed to give me a verbal lashing. That's what you did the last time I caught you checking out my merchandise."

My mouth drops open.

"Your merchandise? Are you selling something now?"

Quinn winks. "That depends on who is buying."

And he saunters out.

Yes, saunters. There is no other word to describe the casual, cocky way that he moves through life. OhMyGod.

My fingers are practically shaking as I pick up my phone and text Gavin. I don't know why I'm shaking, either. I have no idea why I let Quinn affect me like he does. It's like my hormones are instantly nervous whenever he is near. I wonder if his are affected the same way? I shake my head and focus on my phone.

Wanna go diving?

I text this to Gavin. And then I add a smiley face.

There is an answer in less than ten seconds.

My, aren't we happy today? And of course, Mi. The answer to that is always yes.

I shove my phone in my pocket and sigh. So, apparently, I don't usually use emoticons. I should make a list of all the things I don't normally do. But then again, that would negate my new theory that I'm going to rediscover myself. So I shelve that idea.

My phone buzzes in my pocket, so I pull it back out.

BTW, you always wear a bikini to dive. A skimpy one.

I laugh out loud. And I'm still laughing when I hear a voice behind me.

"Good morning, sweet one."

I turn to find Marionette gliding into the kitchen. She bends and hugs me and I am truly happy to see her.

"Good morning," I answer as I return her hug. "Do you happen to know… do I have a car here?"

She smiles. "You do have a car. But it isn't here. And honestly, I don't know if it was damaged in the quake. But Darius would be happy to take you anywhere you need to go."

"Thank you," I smile at her.

"He's out in the barn, I think," she tells me before she grabs a loaded breakfast tray, presumably for my mother.

The thought that my mother is up and around puts a spring into my step. I pack a bag with a one-piece swimsuit and duck out before I can accidentally bump into her. I'm guessing that my mother isn't a morning person, either.

But that's just a guess.

I do find Darius in the barn and he is happy to give me a ride, just as Marionette said he would be. He chats casually during the ride into town. The farm truck is bumpy and jostling, but I don't mind. He drops me off at the pier and as I am standing there, I realize something.

I didn't bring any equipment.

I'm an idiot.

And I'm still standing there like an idiot when Gavin finds me.

"Did you bring your bikini?" he asks with a grin. I roll my eyes.

"I'm pretty sure that I don't even own one," I tell him. "But that was a valiant effort."

He laughs. "You know I'm going to take every advantage of this amnesia thing. Just be forewarned."

"Noted," I answer back. It is absolutely impossible to not be happy around Gavin. And that is the truth.

"Where's your stuff?" he asks, glancing down and only seeing my one little bag.

I wince at my own idiocy.

"I was in a hurry to duck out before I ran into my mom, so I forgot it," I admit sheepishly. Gavin throws his head back and laughs.

"Hmm. Just like old times," he says with another chuckle. "Mia's hiding from her mom again. Maybe it's best if we just swim today, anyway. You can get your sea legs back under you."

I nod because that's probably a good idea.

He leads me onto a pristine little boat named *The Shining*. It's immaculate even though many of the surrounding boats have clearly been damaged in the quake. I look at Gavin questioningly.

"We were out on the water when it hit," he told me. "You, me and Quinn. So there was nothing for my boat to get damaged with."

Oh. This was something I didn't know. I was with Gavin and Quinn at the same time? I wonder how that came to pass? But I don't ask. Instead, I take a seat and enjoy the fragrant sea breeze that blows through my hair as Gavin steers through the bay. The sunlight skims the surface of the water and breaks apart into a million prisms of light. It's gorgeous and I sigh happily while I breathe in the salty air.

"You love it out here," he calls to me when we are on open water. "You always have and I know you always will. We've been doing this since we were small."

"Always together?" I ask curiously. He nods.

"Always."

Hmm. I never know now when he is messing with me, but I look at his face and he is distracted by driving and doesn't seem to be kidding. So, Gavin and I are together a lot. That would make sense since he knows me so well.

He kills the motor after a while and the boat floats. Everything is quiet around us except for the water lapping against the fiberglass hull. It's soothing. I lean back in my seat and allow the sun to wash over my face. I decide that I'm never going to shore. So I tell Gavin that.

He laughs.

"You should've mentioned that beforehand and I would've brought some food. You're kind of bitchy when you don't eat."

I open one eye.

"Isn't everyone?"

He laughs again. "Not like you. You once almost ripped my finger off for stealing your candy bar. I thought you were going to punch me in the throat."

I giggle. It doesn't sound like me. But what do I know?

"You probably shouldn't mess with a girl's chocolate," I advise him. He smiles.

"Yeah, I know that now, thanks to you. Now, do you want to swim?"

Gavin looks at me. I eye the water. I know it must be deep out here. Really, really deep.

"I'm not sure if I remember how," I admit to him. "And I still need to change into my suit."

Gavin's eyes start to sparkle. And that's a dangerous sign. I have re-discovered that already.

"That's no problem," he tells me. "I'll turn my back and you can change. And then we'll get into the water together. You can wear a life-jacket."

I narrow my eyes. "No peeking."

He holds his hands up innocently. "I would never. Okay, maybe I would. But I promise that I won't *today*."

He laughs impishly. And I know, deep down, that I wouldn't be overly mad if he did peek. What does that make me? What kind of girl am I, anyway?

I grab my bag and yank my suit out. True to his word, Gavin turns his back. Although, I do catch him trying to steal a glance in the chrome reflection of the boat trim. I laugh in spite of myself. I have never shoved my clothes off of my body as fast as I do right now. Well, I don't think I ever have anyway. I yank my suit up and slide my arms into the arm straps.

"Done!" I announce.

Gavin turns around, his gaze flickers down and then back up. I can't read the expression in his eyes very well, but I'm guessing he is disappointed that there really is no bikini. He doesn't show it, though. Instead, he grabs a bright orange lifejacket and tosses it to me.

"Put this on."

So I do.

And then I peer over the edge of the boat. The water is brilliant blue and fairly clear.

"Are there sharks?" I ask.

Gavin rolls his eyes. "When in the history of your life, have you ever worried about sharks?" He pauses. "Oh, right. You don't remember. Sorry. You don't worry about sharks because you know that you have a greater chance of dying in an airplane crash than you do of getting eaten by a shark. The chances are slim to none."

For some reason, that doesn't make me feel much better.

But it might be because the sea is so vast and I am so unsure about my swimming skills.

Gavin looks at me and grabs my hand.

"Mia, I would never let anything happen to you. You are a very strong swimmer. All you have to do is trust your instincts. And you have a life jacket on. You'll be fine."

I nod and Gavin counts.
On three, we jump over the side.

Chapter Twelve

I feel panicked for a second as the water closes in over my head. I plunge into the sea and for a brief minute before my lifejacket thrusts me back up, I do panic. I kick hard and flail. But then the buoyancy of the orange vest sends me bobbing back to the surface.

I sputter as my head breaks through the water. And then I gulp in a huge mouthful of air. Gavin is still holding my hand and he shakes the water from his hair as he treads water next to me.

"You okay?" he asks in concern. I nod.

"Yep. I just wasn't expecting it to be so cold."

He looks at me strangely. "You really don't remember anything at all, do you?"

I shake my head. "Nope."

I release his hand and kick away from the boat. I love the weightless feeling that I have right now, even though I'm secretly worried that sharks are going to notice my legs kicking and come up and bite one off. I'm kind of fond of my legs. I'd prefer to keep them.

There's nothing out here, not for miles and miles. I scan the horizon and only see blue. I feel freer than

I've felt since I woke up. I tell Gavin that and he smiles.

"That's why you love it out here so much," he confides. "You're free out here. No restrictions, no expectations. Usually, we dive the old wrecks."

At my clueless expression, he adds, "It's a bunch of sunken ships. You love it."

For some reason, for a minute, I get a chill. Thinking of old sunken ships resting against the bottom of the sea with moss and crap growing on them is pretty creepy. And I don't want to swim down there. But of course I don't want Gavin to know that. I don't want to hear *But you used to love it!* even one more time. It's growing a little old.

I seem to do okay paddling, so I decide to try swimming. I stretch my arms out in front of me and stroke, one after the other. Gavin calls after me.

"You're doing great! I knew you wouldn't forget!"

I bury my face in the sea and allow it to wash over me. The cool water seems to wash everything away and I glide effortlessly through the water. I flip onto my back and close my eyes, basking in the sun as I float.

I don't know how long I bob in the water like this, but I decide that I must have fallen asleep for a minute. Because when I open my eyes again, I am way, way away from the boat.

Far.

Away.

And Gavin is lying on the hull of the boat, asleep. I can tell from the way his arm is thrown up over his head and his eyes are closed.

I flip over and suddenly, I'm terrified.

I'm panicky.

The sea is so very vast.

And I'm so very alone.

I scream. I can't help it. And as I do, I accidentally gulp in a huge mouthful of water. Everything that follows is a blur.

I start coughing and flailing my arms and even though I'm wearing a life-jacket, I'm thrashing around like a lunatic. I hear the boat motor start up and then I feel the wake of the boat as it crests up to me. Gavin is next to me and before I know it, he's hauling me over the side of The *Shining*.

I'm in his lap, on the floor of the boat and he is holding me and I am shaking.

OhMyGod.

I'm such an idiot.

I'm such an idiot.

And I must be repeating it out loud, even though I don't mean to, because Gavin is telling me, "No, you're not."

But I am.

I really am.

"I don't know why I got so afraid," I tell him. "I think I had a panic attack." My voice sounds pathetic and I hate it.

Gavin tightens his grip on me, his strong arms are wrapped around me and I suddenly realize that his skin is pressed against mine and it feels really, really good. I push into him harder and clutch him to me.

Because for some insane reason, I'm still unnerved.

"It's okay," he tells me softly. He's stroking my back and I'm trying to catch my breaths like a normal person. "You've been through a lot. I shouldn't have let you float like that alone. You seemed like you were doing fine, so I climbed up onto the boat to watch you and I must have fallen asleep. I'm so sorry. This is my fault, Mi."

I look up at him. He's so sexy and concerned and my heart melts.

"It's not your fault that I'm insane," I tell him firmly. "I don't know why I panicked. I can't even explain it. Everything just all of a sudden felt so big and I felt so small and alone. I guess I kind of freaked out."

Understatement of the year.

Gavin's dark eyes are soft as he stares at me. He brushes a thumb across my cheek and says that he is so very sorry.

"It makes sense, Mia," he tells me. "You can't remember who you are. So you feel sort of alone in the world. And when you fell asleep while you were floating and woke up, the sea felt big. And everything came down on you at once. It's okay. I get it. But you're never alone. I want you to know that. You will always have me. You always have and you always will."

My heart swells until it might burst.

It feels so incredibly, amazingly good to have this beautiful boy tell me that. To know that he has always been my friend, that he knows me inside and out. And then I do something unexpected.

I lean up and kiss Gavin.

On the mouth.

Sweet Angel of Mercy.

His lips are soft and warm from the sun. I can taste the sea on them and I weave my hands into his hair, pulling him closer. He tightens his grip on me and kisses me back; hard, hard, harder. He tastes like fruit and smells like sunshine.

It's really nice.

Wonderful.

Amazing.

My heart is doing flip-flops when I finally pull away.

Gavin stares down at me in shock.

"I've always wondered what that would be like," he admits. "Kissing a firecracker, I mean." I smile.

"And?"

"It's really too difficult to say from just one kiss," he says, his dark eyes twinkling. "We should try it again so that I have more to go on."

He cups my face in his hands and dips his head, his lips meeting mine.

He tastes of butterscotch and man.

Twenty-five beats of my heart later, he pulls away.

"And?" I breathe.

"You'll do," he grins.

I swat at him and he pulls me into his arms, folding me against his chest. It is warm here, where his skin is bathed by the sun. I feel so safe, like he would protect me from anything. But even better, it's like he knows exactly what to protect me from.

"The old you would never have done that," he tells me quietly a few minutes later. I sigh.

"Gavin, you'll never know how tired I am of hearing that," I tell him. I feel him smile against my shoulder.

"I'm just saying it because it is true. As much as I enjoyed that kiss, I'm thinking that maybe we should hold off on doing it again until you remember a little bit more. Just to be on the safe side. I don't want you slicing off any of my important body parts later because you're mad at me for taking advantage of the situation."

I snuggle closer. "Maybe I'm the one who is taking advantage of you," I suggest.

"Oh? How so?" Gavin asks. He shifts my weight so that I am lying more comfortably in his lap. I feel evidence of his 'important body part' jabbing into me, but I pretend not to notice.

"Maybe I'm using you to jog my memory," I answer. I don't open my eyes. It feels too good to keep them closed in the sun.

He laughs. "Well, in that case, feel free to use me in any way that you want. And if you require any of my important body parts for that, say the word. Just remember, I'm always ready."

I smile.

But then, for a second, one second, Quinn's lopsided grin pops into my head and my heart pounds. Why am I in Gavin's lap and kissing Gavin's lips when Quinn has the ability to give me heart palpations?

The answer is pretty clear though.

Because I like Gavin's lips.

And he has the ability to make my heart pound, too.

In a world that is confusing and scary, Gavin is one of the only things that is real and true. He's steady, like a rock, and I so need that right now.

But is that really a good enough reason to be lying in his lap right now? Maybe he was right and we should wait. I sit up.

"Don't do that," Gavin mumbles. "I was just ready to fall asleep again."

I roll my eyes.

"Maybe you're right," I tell him. This pops his eyes wide open.

"What? Say that again. Because you never, ever say that I'm right."

I roll my eyes again.

"You might be right about this. I don't even know who I am. So how in the world could I know what I want? I don't want to screw you over while I'm trying to figure it out. And I definitely, definitely don't want to ruin our friendship. It's the best thing in my life right now."

He arches a dark eyebrow.

"Mi, I've *always* been the best thing in your life."

He laughs and I laugh with him.

"Seriously, though. You're not going to ruin our friendship. You're not going to screw me over, although I think it's cute that you're worried about it. How about this—we'll just play it by ear. We'll do our thing like we always do. And if things develop like they did this afternoon, we'll pursue them. Don't stress about it. You're not supposed to be stressing. Just relax."

I twist around and stare at him.

"Just relax and go with the flow?"

He nods. "Exactly."

I nestle into his chest once again and he tightens his arms around me. The sun beats down on our shoulders, drying my hair and warming my chilled bones. It feels really, really good here with Gavin.

But just as I'm ready to fall asleep in the sun, I see Quinn's face again. I remember what it felt like when he pressed against me as I was riding Titan. And I hear his charming drawl in my head. My heart quickens in response, like it always does.

I have no idea what I'm doing.

That much is clear.

But as Gavin and I nap in the bottom of *The Shining,* curled up in the sun and miles away from our nearest problem, it is easy to put it out of my mind. I'm going to try and do what Gavin suggested.

I'm going to go with the flow.

I only hope I'm flowing in the right direction.

Chapter Thirteen

I text Dante from the pier and let him know that Gavin will be dropping me off in town. But then Gavin decides to join us. So I spend the remainder of the drive wondering how weird it will be to have Quinn and Gavin in one place.

But it turns out to not be weird at all.

They joke back and forth like old friends and I realize that somewhere along the line, they've become friends since Quinn arrived in Caberra. Gavin treats me like he normally would and no one seems to notice that anything is amiss. No one would ever know that I kissed him on his boat and then took a nap in his arms.

No one except for Reece.

At one point, when Gavin hands me a fresh trash sack, his fingers linger over mine just a little too long. I glance up and smile at him at the same exact time that Reece looks my way. I catch her surprised expression and then her knowing grin. But she doesn't say anything.

Yet.

I have a feeling that it will come later.

For now, I enjoy watching my friends. They joke and laugh and rough-house. We're like a little club, tightly-knit and close. I like it. And even though I don't remember, they don't treat me like I'm different. I like that, too.

I look around the little park that we are cleaning and can see vast improvement over what it looked like a scant two hours ago when we arrived. The broken wood and trash has all been picked up and bagged and it once again looks like a place where children would play. It's a good feeling to know that we did this.

We all stand and stare at it for a minute and our five shadows stretch onto the playground, side by side. Quinn's shadow is the tallest and mine is the smallest. The fact that he is standing next to me at the moment accentuates that fact.

"You really are a tiny tot," he says, only to me. His voice is low and quiet and instant warmth floods my nether regions. OhGoodLord. I'm a wanton, wanton girl. Because two hours ago, I was lying in Gavin's lap.

I gulp.

"I can't help my height," I tell him indignantly.

"Nope," he drawls. "No, you can't. I was just wondering, though, how do you fit that much temper into one tiny body, anyway?"

I glare at him. "I don't have a temper."

Everyone cracks up at this, but I don't see the humor.

"I don't," I insist. But no one listens as they gather up all of our things. My look of indignation is lost because no one is looking. I sigh.

"We should go grab some dinner someplace," Dante suggests. "By the time we get anywhere, it will be dinner time. Anyone up for it?"

"I am," Reece says, leaning up to kiss Dante's cheek. He has a dirt smudge there and she wipes it off before she turns to me. "Mia?"

I nod. "Sure. Just let me text my mom and let her know."

Everyone stares.

"What?" I ask as I pull out my phone. "It would be rude not to let her know."

They stare more.

"I must have been a horrible monster," I mutter as I punch the text into my phone and then put it away.

"Not a monster," Reece tells me.
"Just….different."

"Hmmph," I grunt as I swing into Gavin's Land Rover. "Where are we going to meet?" I ask.

Dante rattles off a restaurant in town and Gavin nods. And then Quinn appears in my open door, filling it up with his large frame.

"Do you mind if I catch a ride with you guys?" he asks. I stare at him in surprise. I had just assumed that he would ride with Dante. He grins in their direction.

"They seem like they'd like a little alone time," he says wryly. Reece is holding Dante's hand, laughing up at him and my heart constricts a little bit. I have to admit...I'm a little jealous. They're so *together*. They fit just right. I wonder if I was ever jealous of them before?

But I'm saved from thinking about it because I have to move to let Quinn in. I climb in the backseat.

"You're way too big to fit back here," I tell him. And it's true. He could fit, but he wouldn't be comfortable.

"Thanks, tiny tot," he tells me as he settles into the front. "But we've already had the conversation about how big I am. You just don't remember it." He grins impishly and his eyes meet mine in the mirror of his visor. I have the sudden feeling it wasn't the size of his body that we had talked about. My heart flutters.

"Everyone set?" Gavin asks. And *his* eyes meet mine in the rearview mirror. His are warm and twinkly because he knows a secret. He knows how we spent the afternoon.

OhGoodLord. How do I get myself into these situations?

I have two gorgeous guys staring at me covertly from the front seat, both with hidden meanings and expressions in their eyes.

So I do what any normal girl would do.

I stare at my hands.

The entire way to the restaurant.

It seems to take forever, but we're actually there in twenty minutes. Trust me, though, twenty minutes is a long time to stare at your hands. By the time we get there, I am painfully aware that I need a manicure.

We pile out and I walk between Quinn and Gavin as we meet Dante and Reece at the door.

Because Dante is the Prime Minister's son, we don't have to wait for a table. We are immediately shown to the best table in the house, actually. It's situated in front of huge windows overlooking the sea. It's a beautiful view.

Or it would be if it didn't offer such a clear view of the city, showcasing the damage from the earthquake. Staring at it is unsettling. Surrounded by the serenity of Giliberti House, it is easy to be removed from the devastation that the quake caused. Not so here. It is readily apparent.

There is rubble everywhere, although streets have been cleared. Trees are down and some power lines too, which means that some people are still without power. It's the worst earthquake this country has seen in years and years.

"Wow," Reece breathes as she takes it in. "We don't have earthquakes where I'm from. Kansas has tornadoes, but not hurricanes or earthquakes. I didn't know what to expect when we arrived here. But it's even worse than I thought it would be."

Dante nods solemnly. "We're just happy that power has been restored to almost everyone. It's amazing how we take things like water or power for granted and we can be reminded so quickly of how lucky we are."

He's right and everyone at the table is quiet for a minute, probably reflecting on that very thing. No one at the table, other than me, was really affected by the quake. Their homes are intact, they didn't even lose power and certainly no one else lost their memories. But I'm really happy about that. I wouldn't wish it on anyone.

We order and then chat while we wait for our food. I find that I am famished. And I am slightly fidgety. I'm seated between Gavin and Reece and across from Quinn. Every once in a while, Quinn catches my eye. His gaze is sparkling and mischievous at all times. It's like he is just waiting for something to amuse him.

Every time he stares at me, my cheeks catch on fire.

And Reece notices this, too. She stares at me once, in confusion and then in realization. Not long after, she excuses herself to go to the bathroom.

And then pauses.

"Mia, do you need to go?" From the way she is staring at me, I decide that I'd better go whether I need to or not. I hurry after her and when we reach the bathroom, she turns to me.

"What are you doing?" she demands. "I can see the tension between you and Quinn. And I saw you flirting with Gavin. Seriously flirting, not his usual BS flirting. I'm not trying to interfere, but Mia, you're supposed to be relaxing so that your memory can come back. I don't think that adding complications to your life is exactly what your doctor meant."

Reece means business. Her cheeks are flushed and I think she's ready to stamp her foot or something.

"Calm down," I tell her. "It's not what you think. Or maybe it is. I don't know. I'm so confused. All I know is that they're both sexy as hell. And I like them both for different reasons."

"You never used to like Gavin in that way," she tells me. "Seriously, you didn't. I always wondered why, because he's cute and funny, but you never did. You said it was because you've seen him in diapers."

I stare at her.

"Well, see, that's the thing. I don't remember seeing him in diapers now, so that's no longer a problem. To me, he's a brand new guy who is sexy as hell and twice as funny. I don't remember anything. All I know is that he makes me feel safe. And trust me, right now I really need that."

Reece nods. "I can see where that would be important to you right now. But what about Quinn?"

I smile at the mere thought of Quinn.

"He's sexy as hell, too," I tell her. "What girl wouldn't be interested in him?"

Reece smiles now, knowingly.

"That's true," she admits. "Everyone loves Quinn. Back home, he can't go anywhere without getting a girl's phone number shoved into his pocket."

"Hometown football hero?" I guess. There's just something about him that screams that.

Reece nods. "Pretty much. And back home, Friday night football games are huge. The whole town turns out. Everyone loves Quinn. And the likeable thing about him is that he isn't very conceited about it. He's just a normal guy who happens to be gorgeous. He's always been that way. It's probably why I used to be totally in love with him."

She grins now. And I have to smile, too. Oh, to be her. Going from being in love with Quinn to Dante. Rough life. I mention as much to her and she grins again. Every time she smiles, her eyes sparkle. I like it. She's ornery-sweet, not ornery-bad ass like

I'm told that I am. Maybe it's why we get along.
We're opposites.

"Dante is the one for me," she shrugs. "For the
longest time, I thought it was Quinn. But one look at
Dante pretty much changed that. You were here
when it happened. You just don't remember it."

I sigh.

"What are you going to do?" she asks me now.
She glances in the mirror and messes with her blonde
hair, pushing one tendril behind her ear. "I've never
seen Gavin actually serious about someone. I've seen
him with a lot of girls, but they were never girls he
would like to keep. You're different. You have to
know that."

I sigh again. Because I think I do know that. I
know it from the tender tone he had in his voice on
his boat. I know it from the soft expression he has in
his eyes when he looks at me. I know it from his
smile. And I know that I never, ever want to hurt
him.

"I don't know what to do," I admit. "I really
don't."

Reece turns to me.

"I think you should just wait it out," she tells me
wisely. "Go on with life and deal with things as they
come. Maybe you should just hang out with both of
them and see what happens. I think that's what I
would do."

My shoulders slump. I can't help it. I'm not good at waiting. Hence my hatred for the words *soon* and *eventually*. Reece wraps an arm around them, bolstering me up.

"It's going to be fine," she announces. "Seriously. You're an amazing, funny, sweet person. Everything will work out for you."

I raise an eyebrow.

"Sweet? You're the first person who has described me in that way."

She giggles. "You *are* sweet. It's deep down because you try to hide it. But you are a sweet person, Mia. And those of us who know you, know that."

"Then you're the only ones who matter," I tell her stoically. "The ones who know me, I mean."

"Exactly," she nods. "We're the only ones who matter. Family doesn't have to mean blood, Mi. We're your family. And even though your parents give you a hard time, they love you, too. They just don't understand you."

I nod. And there is a hard lump that has swelled in my throat and I don't even know why. Reece hugs me again.

"Wanna go back out?"

I nod, not trusting my voice.

And when we walk out to the table, I am surprised to find Elena draped over Quinn's arm.

Her voice is stickily sweet and her boobs are pressed against him.

Instant rage rushes through me, hot and red, but I tamper it down.

Quinn doesn't belong to me.

He's not mine.

But my heart doesn't seem to realize that.

Elena glances up and sees me, then sees Reece. Her expression changes drastically as she locks eyes with Reece. She turns into an ice-bitch directly in front of my eyes.

"Hey, farm girl," Elena says coolly. "I didn't know you were back in town."

I start to interrupt, but Reece speaks first. "And I didn't expect to find you draped across my table."

Elena smiles, her gaze tunneled on Reece. "I'm not. I'm draped across your ex-boyfriend. Jealous?"

She glances my way now and I feel frozen in place. This isn't the girl who I spoke with in the hospital. But if I'm honest, I knew that she had this potential for bitchiness. I could sense it. And now she seems poised to strike, like a snake.

Dante breaks in, though, his voice calm yet cool.

"Leni," he says warningly. I glance at him and he is staring at her, waiting. Expectant. He knows her. He has known her for a long time, so he is patient. Elena looks from him, to Reece, to me.

And then she smiles.

"Hi, Mia," she says, her voice sweet now. "It's good to see you. Would you like to come sit at our table?" She motions to her table, which is crowded with a bunch of other girls our age. They are snickering as they watch this exchange. And I realize that there is no place I'd rather be less.

I shake my head. "No, thanks. I'm fine here."

Elena narrows her green eyes. "Are you sure about that? It might be better for you over there."

My temper snaps to life.

"How so?" I answer, my own green eyes narrowing. Elena smiles wolfishly.

"You're the one who said you wanted to be friends," she reminded me. "I told my girls that and they didn't believe me. If you don't sit with us, they'll think I was lying."

I can feel the incredulous gazes of everyone at the table. All of them are trained on my face, all of them are waiting for me to speak.

I swallow.

"Elena, I'm happy to try and be your friend. But I won't be manipulated or used as a pawn. Ever. So, right now, I'm going to stay here and eat my dinner."

I stare into her eyes and she stares into mine.

And then she smiles, relenting.

"Okay," she says casually. As though it is no big deal at all, as if she is used to people turning her down. "If you change your mind, though, we're over there."

She slides her slender hand along Quinn's shoulders as she leaves and I want to break it. She smiles down at him.

"Call me," she tells him.

I see a piece of paper in his hand and I have to assume it is her number.

My blood boils and I think my vision blurs for a second.

"See you later, D!" she calls to Dante over her shoulder.

Elena is barely gone for a second before Reece marches over to Quinn and yanks the paper from his hand. She tosses it into the burning candle in the center of the table. We all watch it burn.

"Not in this lifetime, Quinn," Reece says. "She's an utter bitch. You don't need that."

Quinn grins, lazy and slow. "Thanks for looking out for me, Reecie," he says. He looks amused. But his words stir something in me. And I freeze.

"Reecie Piecie," I murmur. I am stunned because it triggers something in my brain. Something familiar.

Reece stares at me. "Yes," she says excitedly. "Everyone calls me that. Do you remember?"

And for a second, I do. I see flashes of Reece and me. We're on the water, snorkeling, I think. She's screaming, then laughing. The sun is shining on the water and Dante is there. We're floating and it is peaceful and quiet and I can see why I loved the water. In my head, Reece grabs my hand and the three of us are floating in a circle.

And then the memory stops. I can't remember anything else.

But I have this piece now, this fragment of my past.

And that's something.

I nod.

"I remembered something," I tell them. I sit down and share it. Dante grins.

"I remember that day," he announces. "You were teaching Reece to snorkel. And I pretended to be a shark and scared the crap out of her."

Reece smacks at him now. "I'm still not over that!" she sniffs. "You were a jerk."

"But you love me anyway," Dante tells her, rubbing at his arm. She smiles up at him.

"That's because you're not normally a jerk," she clarifies. Dante is still rubbing his arm.

Gavin looks at me. "Was that all you remembered?"

And I think he's really asking, *Do you remember anything about me?*

I nod. "That's all. But I think it's good. A memory came back. So that means that they aren't all gone forever. Maybe the rest will come back too."

And while everyone else seems encouraged, Gavin seems a little pensive. And I think I know why. He's afraid that if I remember how I felt about him before, I'm not going to feel the same about him as I do right now.

And that's a very valid concern.

I'm worried about the same thing, even while Quinn is staring at me from across the table with such a stormy dark expression. The sexual tension between him and I practically crackles and I want to leap over the table into his arms.

And then Gavin casually lays his arm over the back of my chair and his thumb rubs circles lightly on my shoulder. I glance into his eyes and I find such kindness there, such pure friendship amidst the sparkling dark depths and I gulp.

I don't know what, or who, I want.

I am a mess of utter, swirling confusion.

At this point, I honestly don't know if I want my old memories back or if I wish they'd stay gone forever.

As I look around the table, at the laughing and friendly faces of my friends, I'm beginning to realize that my life is pretty good right now. I might not know what I want, but I'm pretty sure that I don't want anything to change.

At all.

And I know that my memories have the potential to change everything.

Chapter Fourteen

My bedroom has a private balcony. I think all of the bedrooms here at Giliberti House do. I'm sitting on mine tonight, alone, under the dark sky filled with twinkling stars. The night air is cool and it brushes over my skin softly, like tropical velvet fingers.

And I'm feeling nostalgic and poetic.

I don't know why.

There is a book lying open in my lap. It feels good to lose myself in someone else's world tonight, someone else's fictional drama. Because my own drama is too real and raw.

There is a knock on my bedroom door, soft and light. And before I can call out, the door opens and Reece is there. She's wearing pajamas and holding a small box.

"I brought you something," she announces as she crosses my room and joins me on the balcony. "You love these. They're good for anything that ails you. You bought them for me when I was here this summer."

She thrusts the box into my hands and I peer inside.

Tiny chocolate volcanoes sit amidst tissue.

I raise an eyebrow.

"Chocolate therapy?"

"Is there a better kind?" she tosses back.

"Excellent point," I answer. I pop one into my mouth and then I almost melt into my seat. "Oh my gosh. Yummo."

Reece looks satisfied. "Right? I braved the scary gypsy lady for you. That's how much I love you."

"Scary gypsy lady?" This intrigues me. Reece sighs.

"The woman in town who sells these is terrifying," she tells me. "You laugh about her, but she's got these cloudy eyes that see right through a person. And she always mutters vague things about people, as if she can see our future. Last time I was here, she told me that I was strong enough to handle anything. It was like she knew what was going on in my life. It was creepy."

"Were you?" I ask. "Strong enough?"

Reece looks at me, gorgeous in her blonde, girl-next-door way. She finally nods.

"Yes. I was. And I am. It's something I learned while I was here. Everyone is strong enough. Sometimes, they just don't know it. You're strong enough too."

"You're very profound, you know that?" I nudge her jokingly. But honestly, I'm not joking. Reece has given me some pretty good advice so far.

I look at her. "So, I guess my best friend is a sage, then."

She laughs. "I don't know about that. But you've never steered me wrong, either, so I guess we're good for each other."

I offer her a chocolate.

"Thank you for being my friend," I tell her sincerely. "Thank you for sticking with me even when I don't remember how good of a friend you actually are."

Reece looks at me like I've suddenly grown two heads.

"Seriously? That's what friends do. You would do the same for me."

I honestly hope that is true, that I'm a good enough person for that.

We lean back onto our chairs and stare at the stars. Reece wraps her sweater more tightly around her and then pulls something from her pocket.

"I almost forgot," she tells me. She hands it to me.

A picture in a silver frame.

It's Dante, Gavin and me, and we're standing in front of the sea. Sunshine bathes our bare shoulders and we're wearing swimsuits. I have blue and green stripes in my dark hair, an interesting, peacock-like combination. It's clear that we are having a good time because we're all laughing. It's a candid shot, not posed. Gavin's eyes are twinkling and he's bending toward me. Dante is laughing at us.

And I wish I could remember the joke.

But I don't.

Reece watches me and I feel my lips curve into a smile, simply from the happy expression on my face in the picture.

It makes me feel warm inside.

"Dante had this, so I had a copy made for you and framed. It was from a beach party this past summer. I love it. In fact, I love it so much that I had a copy made for me, too."

"Thank you," I tell her sincerely. "Very much. It's like you've handed me a piece of my life, like I have a glimpse of who I was through this picture. I love it."

Tears well up in my eyes and I don't know why. I wipe at them impatiently.

Reece looks at me sympathetically.

"It's okay to be upset," she tells me. "Anyone would be. And you're handling it so much better than most people would. Cut yourself some slack, Mi."

And her words make me cry.

It's like the barrier that I've built around myself lately crumbles down and I gulp at the air, sucking at it like a fish on a sidewalk as I heave in wracking sobs.

At first Reece is shocked, then she grabs me and pulls me to her. She pats my back and murmurs soothingly to me as I cry. And surprisingly, it feels good. When I'm finally finished and I'm lying in Reece's lap, I feel cleansed. It's like my tears washed my anxiety away.

At least, temporarily.

And I decide that if Gavin was right and I never cry, I might change that. A good cry every once in a while might be a good thing. A cleansing thing.

But I do feel bad for falling apart on Reece.

"I'm sorry," I tell her. "I didn't mean to fall apart on you."

She rolls her eyes. "Do you know how many times I've fallen apart on you? Trust me, I owe you a few breakdowns."

I smile and nod like I know, even though we both know that I don't.

"You know what you need?" Reece asks. "You need some ice cream. With fudge and marshmallows. And then a bubble bath. Come on."

I follow her from my bedroom, down the stairs and into the kitchen. There's a soft nightlight shining in there, like a golden beacon. I love this kitchen. It's warm and cozy, definitely a room where a family thrives. I don't know why I'm drawn to it like I am.

But it practically feels like the pulse of this large house beats from this room.

Reece pulls things from the cupboard and drags a couple kinds of ice cream from a large freezer.

We make two of the biggest ice cream sundaes in the history of the world and then make our way out to the terrace. We eat our ice cream curled up on elaborate wrought iron chairs and surrounded by fragrant flowers.

"I love it here," Reece tells me with a sigh. "Everything is so beautiful. I'm going to lobby hard to finish our senior year here. We're needed here anyway."

I look at her, at my friend who seems to have such a big heart. She's innocently licking her spoon when I hear a deep voice from behind me.

Quinn.

"Is this a party and I wasn't invited?"

He asks this as he saunters into the gardens. I think he saunters everywhere. There's simply no other way to describe the way he moves. It's fluid and confident.

And sexy.

"Nope," Reece tells him. "But I guess it is now. Isn't it always a party when you're around?" She grins at him and their manner is relaxed and easy, like two people who have grown up together, because that's exactly who they are. They both have the same charming American accent and the same friendly way about them.

"It's so strange that you guys didn't end up together," I tell them. Reece looks over at me, startled, while Quinn laughs.

"Did you hear that, Reecie? I told you that we were perfect together."

He's kidding though and it is apparent. They are relaxed and friendly, but there is no sexual chemistry between them at and it's hard to imagine that there ever was. Quinn nudges her shoulder, but he sits in the chair next to me. Something inside of me is happy about that, satisfied. I can smell him on the breeze, an outdoorsy man smell. I like it.

Reece rolls her eyes.

"I can't date Quinn," she tells me. "Because we know everything about each other. For example, I know that he passed out when he was giving blood last year." She laughs again and Quinn glowers at her.

"For the last time," he tells her. "The doctor said that there was a real medical reason for that—a vaso-vagal nerve reflex or something."

Reece giggles. "Whatever, little kittie," she laughs. "Meow!"

I'm staring at her, wondering why the heck my seemingly sane friend is meowing at Quinn when she catches a glimpse of my face and laughs harder.

"It's a nice way of calling him a pussy...cat." She tacks the last word on as an afterthought. And then I have to laugh. Because the P-word coming out of sweet little Reece's mouth in any context just doesn't seem right.

And then I meow at Quinn too, just because it is funny to associate him with the P-word in any way, shape or form.

So that is how Dante finds us a few minutes later.

Reece and I are leaned together, meowing at big, strong Quinn under the light of the moon. We look like lunatics, I'm sure. And we most certainly sound like it. But I don't even care. I grin up at Dante.

"Hey, D," I smile.

Dante smiles back, then startles.

"D?"

I look at him for a second, startled too, before I shrug. "It's probably because I heard Elena call you that earlier."

I'm not sure, though. It could be a memory. I have no idea. But I'm distracted by listening to Reece complain about how Elena apparently calls Dante "D" just to annoy her now, and then by listening to her lecture Quinn on the fact that he needs to stay far, far away from Elena because she is a mean witch who would probably eat kittens for breakfast if she could, raw and with the fur still on.

They both listen to her patiently.

And then patiently ignore her.

Apparently, they're accustomed to her funny little outbursts.

Dante wraps an arm around Reece's shoulders and turns to me.

"Mia, are you settling in all right? Is your room okay?"

I nod. "I love my room and the balcony. Thank you so much for letting us stay here."

Dante waves his hand. "I'm glad you're here. It's like a party. Well, it would be if Gavin were here, too."

Gavin.

Immediately, thoughts of him flood my mind and I feel guilty for sitting here with Quinn and I don't know why. Neither of them belong to me. And I don't answer to either of them. Yet whenever I'm with one, I feel guilty about the other. I sigh. My life is complicated.

Dante is tugging at Reece. "I think it's time for bed," he tells her. "We've had a long day and you haven't been sleeping well."

"That's because I'm jet-lagged," she tells him, somewhat grumpily. He smiles patiently.

"I know, little Sunflower," he tells her. "And you get grumpy when you're jetlagged. That's why you should go to bed now. You'll feel better in the morning."

She growls, but it is a harmless, delicate growl. I give her a hug and tell her good night and then they are gone. Quinn and I are the only ones left and I stare at him.

"So, you really passed out when they took your blood?" I ask curiously. I'm trying to imagine this giant of a boy fainting. His hands are so big that it seems like he could palm my head if he wanted to.

He grins ruefully.

"I went down like a rock," he admits. "Does that ruin your macho image of me?" He's still grinning, totally unconcerned. He knows that it doesn't ruin anything for me. If anything, it makes me like him even more.

If that is possible.

But I tell him exactly the opposite.

"Of course it does," I tell him laughingly. "I'll never look at you the same."

He is unconcerned as he moves closer to me. I take a whiff of his shirt as he leans in. Big mistake, because now I can't concentrate on what he is telling me. His man-smell has my hormones tap-dancing.

"Well, do you want to?"

Quinn is looking at me and I have no idea what he asked me. My attention was distracted by my stupid tap-dancing hormones.

"I guess," I tell him, secretly praying that I'm not agreeing to do something horrible.

He looks at me in amusement. "Well, don't get too excited. But I think a walk would do you some good, out here in the fresh air. And of course, there's me. I would do you good, too."

I suck in my breath and he laughs.

My hormones do jazz hands.

And then Quinn pulls me to my feet.

We walk through the gardens and I can't help but notice that he hasn't let go of my hand. His is huge and strong and has callouses on the fingers. My heart speeds up; fast, faster, faster until I can hear it roaring in my ears. As he guides me over a loose stone tile, I am pressed against him and I stare up at him, his eyes frozen on mine.

Time seems to stop.

I can count my heart beats.

Everything is a blur.

He bends his head.

His lips meet mine.

My mind gets blown.

For real.

He pulls away and stares down at me, his gaze intense and dark and smoldering.

Yes, smoldering.

I urge myself to remember to breathe.

He grins. And my knees weaken.

"So, you don't feel the need to meow now? I'm not a pussy...cat now?"

"No. You're more like a lion," I tell him.

Then I grin and kiss him again. We kiss for quite a while, actually, until my hands are clutching his back and I am gasping for breath.

When Quinn finally pulls away, he looks satisfied.

"Ready to walk?" he asks casually, as though he hasn't just addled every wit that I have by playing tongue twister in my mouth. I nod silently, not really trusting my voice.

Quinn is a fantastic kisser.

That much is true.

We walk in the moonlight for a half hour or so. Quinn tells me everything that he's learned about the estate since he's been here, things that I should know but don't. He shows me the building where I normally work. He shows me the factory buildings where the gourmet olive oils are made. And then we make the long walk back to the house.

I walk slowly because I don't want the evening to end.

He walks me to my room and kisses me yet again.

And I definitely don't want him to leave, but obviously he has to.

After I go inside my bedroom, I have to lean against the door for quite a while before my shaking knees feel strong enough to walk to my bed.

I meow at myself.

Because I totally deserve it.

Chapter Fifteen

I dream about Quinn.

And then I dream about Gavin.

Why do they both have to be such amazingly awesome kissers?

Why do I have to be so freaking indecisive?

Why is my heart so clueless?

Oh My Word.

When I wake in the morning, the sunshine is cheerful, but I'm not. Because I feel like an utter loser. I kissed two sexy guys in one day. And I honestly don't know which kiss I enjoyed more. There's clearly something wrong with me.

I jump in the shower and then get dressed.

And then I text Reece.

Want to go into town with me?

She answers back immediately. *Sure. Where are we going?*

To fix my hair, I text her.

She answers with a smiley face and *I'll be there in five.*

Reece is literally in my room in five minutes. She looks at me and smiles. She looks fresh and cute in a pair of cut-off jean shorts, pony-tail, snug t-shirt and a pair of cowboy boots.

Yep. Cowboot boots.

With shorts. And she totally pulls it off.

"What color are you thinking?" she asks as we wind our way downstairs.

"I don't know," I muse. "Pink?"

She grins again. "Pink has always suited you."

My mother is in the dining room having breakfast and I bend and kiss her cheek. I ignore the startled look on her face and tell her that I'm going to town.

"We'll be back in a bit!" I tell her over my shoulder. She's still too surprised by my display of affection to say anything.

Reece has Dante's keys to his fancy Maserati. I decide he must love her a *lot* to let her drive this car. It has so many bells and whistles that I can't even figure all of the buttons out. I settle into the passenger seat as Reece drives the curvy roads into Valese. I also commend her on figuring out all of the buttons on this dashboard.

"I grew up driving farm trucks," she tells me conversationally. "It took a while to get used to driving Dante's car because it's just so nice. But that's not a problem that you have. Your little car is really nice, too. And it's what you learned to drive on. You never had to learn on a three-on-the-tree old truck."

"Three-on-the-tree?" I ask. She nods.

"It's an old fashioned stick shift. You shift the gears on a shifter on the steering column, instead of on the floor. But once you learn on something like that, you can pretty much drive anything," she tells me cheerfully. "So it was probably a good thing."

"I don't know if I'll remember how to drive," I tell her. "I haven't tried since the accident."

"That's okay," she answers. "We'll go get your car later and give it a try."

I smile at her because she really is trying to make my life normal. She doesn't even act afraid to be the one with me when I try to drive. She's brave. So I tell her that. She laughs.

"No, brave is waking you up before 10:00 a.m. Driving with you was always a little terror-inducing, so I'm used to it already."

I roll my eyes and laugh and we're in town before I know it.

I stare out my window, watching the buildings that pass by. I keep thinking that if I look at things that I should know hard enough, I'll recognize them. It hasn't happened yet, though. Reece parks and we stroll down the main strip. Cute boutiques line each side of the cobblestone street. People swarm in loosely woven crowds on the walk. I feel like some of them stare at me.

"Do you think they know me?" I ask Reece. She shrugs.

"Probably. I'm sure they know who you are."

It's hard to ignore the stares, but I give it my best shot.

"I wonder how much money I have?" I muse curiously. "I mean, I have a credit card in my purse, but I don't know how much I can spend on it."

Reece giggles. "I don't think it's something you have to worry about," she answers. "You used to go on crazy shopping sprees and never even blinked. I'm pretty sure you just use your credit card and then your dad pays the bill."

I nod. "Okay." That seems awfully nice of my father. I'll have to remember to thank him.

Reece pulls me into a trendy little shop and I find several cute outfits. Leggings and mini-skirts, flowing shirts, chunky jewelry. I can't decide which one to get, so I get them all. I need clothes anyway. Most of mine were destroyed in the quake and I don't like what my mom bought for me. I never knew there were so many shades of beige in the world.

Reece looks over my haul in amazement.

"What?" I raise an eyebrow. She shakes her head.

"Nothing. There's just not one black thing in the bunch."

That *is* interesting. "I guess maybe I didn't like wearing black so much as I liked the reaction I got from it," I muse. "I don't know. But I don't feel the urge to buy it now."

"That's fine," Reece assures me. "You should buy what you want. And apparently, your gut is telling you to buy a lot of hot pink."

I smile. "I want to accessorize with my hair. Which reminds me, we need to go have that done." I keep one of my new outfits on, complete with a cute pair of canvas sneakers and fingerless gloves. I feel trendy and sort of skater-chic.

Reece leads me out and down the street to a little spa. I don't have an appointment, but once I tell them my name, they fit me right in. Apparently, Dante's not the only one around here that gets special treatment. Hmm. Perhaps being the daughter of the Minister of Defense comes in handy. Except for when people stare at me in public, that is.

Within a couple of hours, my hair is two shades darker with hot pink streaks threaded through it. I stare in satisfaction in the mirror.

"I love it," I assure my stylist. "It seems so cheerful and happy."

Reece smiles at me. "You look like yourself again—but with different clothes. I love the new look, Mia."

"So do I," I tell her happily. "I feel like I'm on the way to figuring out who I am. Whoever said retail therapy doesn't work is insane."

"I agree. It works like a charm for me every time. Are you hungry? There's a bunch of little bistros and cafes down the street."

I nod. "I'm famished. Spending money apparently works up an appetite."

She links her arm through mine and we make our way to a little area on the other end of the street that is surrounded by restaurants. There is an open air seating area in the middle, apparently shared by all of the bistros. We grab a sandwich and then head for a table.

And as we walk, I hear a tinkling, familiar laugh.

I turn my head and find Elena.

And she is sitting on Gavin's lap.

I freeze, my feet unable to continue walking.

Elena is perched delicately against Gavin's chest and she is giggling into his ear. He is laughing too, because Gavin is almost always laughing. He seems perfectly happy to have her on his lap, pressed against him. He is definitely not making any move to get her off. He seems to be enjoying himself, actually.

Reece is staring too.

"Um…" she stutters. She has no idea what to say.

"It's okay," I tell her. "Seriously. I don't own him."

But it feels like someone has impaled my heart. And I don't even know why. I truly don't own him. He owes me no explanations. But it feels like he just yanked my heart out and drop-kicked it.

I head over in their direction.

"Mia, you have to keep in mind, Gavin is different than us. He's so easy-going. He pretty much goes with the flow in any situation. I'm sure he's thinking nothing of this."

Reece has found her tongue now. I nod, but I'm not really listening. Instead, I march up to the table next to them and set my tray down. Gavin is startled and then surprised and I can tell that he is really wishing now that Elena wasn't on his lap.

Tough crunch.

She is, so he needs to answer for it.

Okay. Maybe I've changed my mind. I guess I do want an answer.

But I don't ask for it. Instead, I smile cheerfully at them.

"Hey, guys. What's up?"

Gavin doesn't push Elena off, but instead, he leans around her to talk to me.

"I like the hair," he tells me with a grin. "I just bumped into Elena and she decided to sit with me."

"You mean, *on* you?" I correct him. His smile falters. He can see that I'm annoyed.

Elena chooses to move now and she smiles at me. I can't see anything malicious in her smile, although I might be wrong.

"Hi, Mia," she tells me. She completely ignores Reece.

"Hi," I answer.

But honestly, I'm not really interested in anything she has to say. She looks gorgeous today, as usual. She's got a revealing tank top on that plunges to a low V in the front and in the back. I love the shirt. I just wish that she didn't look so perfect in it while she was on Gavin's lap. Her hair and make-up is perfect, as always, and truly, you can barely see the scar on her cheek now.

Gavin hands me a little boutique bag.

"I got you a gift. I hope you like it," he says.

And his voice *is* hopeful. I'm not sure if he's hopeful that I'm not mad for finding Elena on his lap or if he's hopeful that I'll simply like his gift. And Reece might actually be right. He doesn't seem unsettled at all that I found them like this. Maybe he really didn't think anything of it.

But that's a little unsettling to me.

Because I don't like it. It's okay to be friends with members of the opposite sex. But if you like someone else, you really shouldn't have other girls sitting on your lap.

That's just my opinion.

However, I don't voice that right now. Instead, I peer into the bag and see a white oblong box. I lift it out and pull off the box top and find a silver watch. It is relatively simple and slender, with a feminine band and a diamond on the 12 and the 6. It's gorgeous.

"It's inscribed," Gavin tells me. I flip the watch over and on the back it reads *It's always Gavin Time.*

I forget my agitation with him momentarily and laugh. I can't help it. He's so completely arrogant, but charmingly so. He makes it so hard to stay mad.

"It's beautiful," I tell him. "Thank you."

I start to put it on, but Gavin shoves my hand away and fastens it for me. And then he lifts my hand to his lips and kisses it. He lets his lips linger on my skin, warm and soft. And he's staring into my eyes and anyone in the vicinity can feel the atmosphere change around us. It's sexually charged.

I know it.

Reece knows it.

And Elena certainly knows it. I can see the interest on her face now and I doubt that's a good thing. She has a strange smile pasted on her face as she watches us. But I'll worry about that later.

For now, I've got other things to worry about.

Like how to stay mad at Gavin.

But that turns out to be an exercise in futility. He has me snapped out of my anger within ten minutes and we sit and chat with him for at least an hour more. Elena pretends that Reece doesn't exist, and Reece keeps her back to Elena. But other than that, everything feels normal.

Gavin has the ability to make anyplace feel like a party. We're laughing and joking and talking to the strangers sitting around us and I feel infinitely at peace.

That is, until Elena gets up to leave. She tells me goodbye, ignores Reece and then she bends to kiss Gavin on both cheeks in the normal European fashion. But her kisses linger. And her hands brush over his chest. Then she pushes her boobs against him. And when she turns, her eyes meet mine and I see something unsettling there, lurking beneath the fake friendliness and sparkling emerald depths.

A challenge.

Chapter Sixteen

"I don't know what to do," I tell Reece on the way home. "I just don't know what to do. I love so many things about Gavin. I love how he knows me. I love how he gets me. I love how he makes everyone feel so comfortable at any given time. But that same exact thing is a curse, too. Look at this episode with Elena. Rather than push her off his lap, he rolled with the punches and ate it up. Would he be that same way if we dated? Because I wouldn't be okay with random girls sitting on his lap."

Reece glances at me. "Okay, is it time for me to answer you now? Because I've tried four times and you haven't stopped talked long enough for me to get a word in edgewise."

I smile sheepishly. "I know. I think I must chatter when I'm nervous."

"You do," she confirms. "But in answer to your monologue, this is just what Gavin is like. You're right about all of the traits that you just named. And he is very loyal to his friends. That's something else positive about him. And honestly, I have no idea what Gavin is like with a girlfriend. He's always been a player- or ever since I've known him, anyway. He's never been serious enough to get involved with a girl for any amount of time. He's accidentally left a long trail of broken hearts behind him."

I slump against the seat. "This isn't helping."

Reece stares at me sympathetically for a minute before she watches the road again. "I'm sorry. It's a hard choice. They've each got pretty great qualities."

"Can you tell me more about Quinn?" I ask. "I mean, something that you haven't told me yet?"

Reece thinks about it for a minute.

"Well, he's loyal, too. He dated my friend Becca for years. And even though most of the girls in school had it bad for him, he never cheated on her. Ever. He's good at everything he does. He rides bulls in competitions with Becca's brother, Connor. And he wins. And of course, he's a good football player. He'll probably go to college on a football scholarship. He loves animals, also. He wants to be a veterinarian."

"So, he must have a big heart," I muse. Reece nods.

"Very big," she tells me. "I remember our freshman year. We had this really small kid in our freshman class. He was always getting picked on by the upperclassmen football players. They kept shoving him into trashcans in the locker room, or closing him in lockers. You know, stupid Neanderthal jock crap. Well, one day, Quinn found the kid, Mike, in the office getting an ice pack from the nurse. Apparently, when the older boys shoved him into a locker that day, they had broken three of his fingers. Quinn took care of it the next day."

"How?" I ask.

"Quinn started walking everywhere with Mike. Through the halls, sitting with him at lunch, etc etc. And when the upperclassmen still tried to give Mike crap, Quinn told them they'd have to go through him first if they wanted to keep messing with Mike. And they didn't want to. Quinn was a big bruiser even as a freshman."

"What happened to Mike?" I ask.

Reece smiles.

"Well, Mikey is now Quinn's best friend in the world. He actually had a growth spurt so he's a bit taller than he was. Quinn got him playing ball and now he's our quarterback, actually. And he *never* bullies the freshman the way he was bullied."

"That's a nice story," I tell her. "I bet Mike will pay it forward. He'll probably do nice things for other people because he'll always remember how nice Quinn was to him."

Reece nods. "He's already paid it forward, tons of times. He's a good guy. Just like Quinn. Quinn is the kind of guy that makes you want to be a better person. He's got such a... good soul. I don't know how else to describe it. He's got a pure heart, through and through."

"I can see that about him," I admit to her. "I really can."

"So, please, Mi. Don't hurt him. I know he seems like a player. And he's inadvertently broken a few hearts, but he didn't mean to. I would really hate to see him get hurt, even if it was on accident."

"What should I do?" I whisper to her as we turn onto the Giliberti property. She shakes her head.

"I don't know."

"What would *you* do?" I ask.

She shakes her head again. "I don't know. I'm horrible at this stuff."

I sigh. "What good are you?" I tease. She shrugs.

"Well, I always know when to bring you chocolate."

"True. That's a good enough reason alone to keep you."

As we pull up into the circular drive in front of the house, I see Quinn sitting on the huge wrap-around porch with Dante. They appear to be deep in conversation and they are laughing. That's a good sign. And truly, there should be a law or something against two such good-looking boys being in one spot. They make it hard to concentrate.

As we cross the lawn to them, they look up and see us and both grin at the same time. I think the heavens open up and the angels sing.

Okay, that might be an exaggeration. But that's definitely what happened in my head. Their smiles are just that gorgeous and bright. And Quinn's is sexily crooked.

"Hey girls!" Dante calls out. "Did you leave anything in the stores or did you buy it all?"

We *are* carting a lot of bags. I am woman enough to admit that.

The boys get up and help us carry it into the house. As they do, Quinn turns to me.

"You look really pretty," he tells me. "I'm glad the stripes are back."

His eyes are sparkling mischievously, but his expression is sincere.

"Thank you," I tell him. "I feel more like myself. I think."

He laughs. "You've definitely got your swagger back," he tells me. Dante turns around in front of us.

"I was just saying that we should have a beach party tonight to try and forget about our stress for a bit. What do you think?"

"I'm all for it," Quinn chimes in. Reece laughs.

"Quinn, you've never met a party yet that you didn't like," she accuses laughingly. He doesn't deny it. Instead, he helps me carry my bags to my room.

As we walk in, he looks around. I'm thankful that I didn't leave any panties lying around.

"See something you like?" I ask teasingly. He grins.

"Maybe," he answers. "What do you think about the beach party tonight?"

Short pause. He stares at me. I have no idea what he's waiting for.

I shrug as I drop my bag on the bag.

"It sounds fun," I tell him. "You're going, right?"

He grins. "I've apparently never met a party that I didn't like," he tells me charmingly.

"I can see that about you," I reply. "So, you'll be there?"

He nods. "I wouldn't miss it."

Another long pause.

Then he gives me an ornery gaze and then he's gone.

When Reece and I are ready to leave later in the evening, Dante is waiting for us on the porch. But Quinn is nowhere to be found.

"Where's Quinn?" I ask curiously. Dante shakes his head.

"He left earlier, but he'll meet us there."

"How will he know where to go?" I ask. "He's not that familiar with Valese yet, is he?"

Dante looks amused. "Well, Elena picked him up. So I'm guessing she'll show him the way."

Reece and I both freeze and stare at Dante. He holds his hands up innocently.

"Hey, don't look at me. He's a big boy- he can do what he wants."

Reece narrows her eyes. "But you let him go with her? She's a viper. She'll eat him up for breakfast and then ask for more."

Dante doesn't seem concerned. "I thought she ate kittens for breakfast?" he teases. "Besides, if he's still with her for breakfast, I doubt he'll care if she asks for seconds."

Reece squeals and smacks his arm and I gulp.

I ignore their bantering as I try not to physically cringe. How could Quinn have gone with Elena? Did he not think it was important enough to mention that when I asked him if he was going? Instead of being quiet and staring at me, he could've brought that small fact to my attention.

So apparently, I'm not going to have to choose between Gavin and Quinn. The choice has been made for me.

I'm not sure if I'm relieved about that or not.

I don't think I am.

I try not to think of it as we drive to the beach and then walk over the sandy dunes. The party is far back from the public beaches, secluded on private property. I'm told that I've been to many of these parties. I don't remember a one.

But when we arrive, it looks like a good time.

Tons of kids are already here, laughing and playing around. I don't remember any of them, although I do recognize a few from when they visited me in the hospital.

A group of boys is throwing a ball back and forth. A group of girls is watching. Another co-ed group is splashing in the surf. There are huge containers of beer and wine-coolers buried in ice. There are tables of food, mostly fresh seafood and bread. There are bonfires. And I love the atmosphere here. It's happy and carefree. The flickering bonfires in the dying sunlight provides the perfect ambience for a beach party.

I unfold a chair and sit in it. Reece sticks a wine cooler in my hand.

"Your favorite," she tells me. "Just don't have twelve of them."

She gives me a stern look, making me wonder if I have a drinking problem or something. And then she settles into the chair next to me while Dante gets in on the ball-throwing action. The boys, by this point, are taking off their shirts. And not because it's hot outside, either. Next to the sea, the breeze is actually a bit chilly today, but they're stripping down anyway. I shake my head. The male species is so crazy sometimes.

Dante leaves his shirt on though and Reece shakes her head regretfully.

"There comes a time when that boy needs to let loose with the rest of them," she tells me. "He's so happy to be home, though."

"What about you?" I ask her. "Are you happy to be here instead of home in Kansas?"

Reece picks at the label on her bottle and thinks about that for a minute.

"I love it here," she finally says. "Even though when we were in Kansas, it felt like Dante was removed a bit from the pressures of being who he is, which was good, I think I still love being here more. I mean, of course I miss my mom and Becca and my grandparents, but there's just something about Caberra that made me fall in love with it. Honestly, though, I would be happy wherever Dante is. I know, that sounds corny. But it is true."

And I know that Dante feels the same way. I can see it in the way his gaze seems to find her periodically no matter what he's doing. He checks on her and I think it's sweet. And once again, jealousy rears its ugly head. I really do hope that someday, someone looks at me the way Dante looks at Reece.

Honestly, no sooner have I had that thought when a pair of dark, twinkling eyes meet mine from across a crowd of boys.

Gavin.

He's standing against one of the coolers talking with another boy that I don't know. He's got on a pair of black shorts and a white shirt, unbuttoned at the neck and rolled at the sleeves. He's barefoot and he's gorgeous. He looks like a swimwear model for a European magazine. That's how gorgeous he is.

I smile automatically as his eyes meet mine.

He smiles back.

And my heart flutters like a thousand butterflies.

"Well, well," Reece drawls, watching the silent exchange. "Look who is forgiven."

I roll my eyes at her. "You said it yourself. He didn't mean anything by it. He's a natural flirt. He doesn't want Elena."

I twist my new watch on my arm. I can practically feel his name pressing into my skin. *It's always Gavin Time.* I almost giggle again just thinking it, but then I realize that it's fairly true. I'm always in the mood for Gavin.

That has to say something, right?

I make my way toward him.

He meets me in the middle.

"Hi," he says softly. "Nice bling. Was it a gift?" He motions toward my watch. I smile.

"Yeah. This guy I know gave it to me."

Gavin raises an eyebrow. "Oh, really? Do I need to do some ass-kicking? He seems like a pretty awesome guy. I don't want any competition."

I laugh and he laughs and then he links his arm with mine.

"Let's walk," he suggests.

As we walk away from the crowd and toward the water, I catch sight of Quinn and Elena approaching the party. She is draped over his arm and he looks to be enjoying it. Of course, to be fair, he's a red-blooded guy and her boobs are pressed into his arm. Of course he's going to enjoy it. I swallow hard and try not to plot murderous things against Elena and her boobs.

I'm walking with Gavin, I remind myself.

Quinn and Elena don't matter to me.

But as we pass them and Quinn's eyes meet mine in a smoldering stare, I know that he does matter. A lot.

I fight the urge to turn around and look at him again.

And I win. I don't look.

Take that, self-control.

Somehow, I am able to focus on Gavin and our walk and the beautiful beach. I put Quinn out of my mind. Once or twice, I glance in his direction and find Elena laughing into his ear. Once, his arm is even snaked around her waist and at that, I squeeze my eyes shut and turn away. It's the last time I peek at him.

Gavin looks at me now, a bit of concern on his handsome face.

"Is everything alright?" he asks me. "You seem distracted."

He leads me to a huge piece of driftwood and sits me down. He sits so close that his thigh presses into mine. I like the feeling.

"I'm fine," I lie. "It's weird, knowing that I've been to a bunch of these parties and I don't remember any of them. Not a thing."

Gavin studies me for a second. Then he brushes a thumb against my cheek. His eyes are soft as he stares into mine.

"Want me to help?" he asks quietly. "I can tell you what you normally do at these parties."

I stare at him for a moment. I know that whatever is going to come out of his mouth will be utter bullshit but I can't stop myself. I nod.

"Okay. What do I usually do?"

Gavin stares out to sea for a minute, then turns back to me, picking up my hand.

"Well, first you usually eat dinner with me. We grab some fresh crab legs because you love them. I have oysters because, well, you know what they say about oysters and the libido. Then, you drink about a dozen wine coolers. And then, at some point in the evening, you get sick. And I spend a chunk of time hunting for someone else to babysit you so that I don't have to hold your hair back while you vomit. That's what usually happens. So, I would suggest not drinking too many tonight."

I shake my head. I guess he really is telling the truth. I was a party girl. Hmm.

"Good advice," I tell him. "So, you need to eat oysters for your libido? Your libido isn't strong enough without an aphrodisiac?"

Gavin stares at me for a second, before he bursts out laughing.

"Touché," he tells me. "Trust me, my libido is healthy and thriving. Also, I forgot to mention one thing that you always, always do at these parties."

And now I know to disregard whatever comes out of his mouth next because his eyes are twinkling, his mouth is curving up. But I still smile and ask what it is.

"You always go skinny-dipping with me," he says impishly. "Always."

It's my turn to burst out laughing now.

"You're crazy," I tell him. "I call bullshit. You're insane."

He nods solemnly. "I know," he tells me, unconcerned. "But you love me anyway."

And I do love him.

I realize that right now. I don't know what way I love him, but I do love him. Whether he's the familiar brother that I never had or ultra-hot boyfriend material remains to be seen. But one way or another, I love him.

It's a startling, yet comforting feeling.

Chapter Seventeen

I restrain myself and only have two wine coolers. I can't imagine drinking any more than that, because honestly, I don't enjoy the taste. But Reece and Dante both seem proud of me for my restraint, so I decide that I definitely must've been a wild party girl of some sort. Gavin had been telling the truth, after all.

Night falls quickly out here overlooking the water and I watch the sun sink down over the horizon in an explosion of gorgeous colors that ricochet off the water and bathe everything in gorgeous light. Reece wraps her arm around my shoulders.

"What do you think, Mi?" she asks. It's an open ended question.

"About what? How the world began? I think it was divine design. About world relations? I think that Caberra is in a good place- both economically and politically. I know the prime minister, so I feel good about that." I'm joking now and Reece rolls her eyes.

"I meant, what do you think about your life?" she says.

"Oh," I answer. "And I thought you were asking a big question."

She laughs now, but she waits for my answer. Because she's my friend, she's actually interested. Drat. I have to give her a thoughtful answer.

Um.

"I don't know," I admit to her. "I honestly don't. I think about it all the time, because I can't help it. I'm constantly wondering how the new me compares to the old me and which one is actually me. It's confusing and exhausting. Like tonight, it would seem that I used to be a party girl. But I honestly don't feel the need to get wild or crazy. It's like I've spun around in a one-eighty from the girl I used to be. And I wonder if it's partially because of the head injury. I mean, will I go back to normal? Or was my old "normal" just a façade? Was I pretending to be someone that I wasn't? I just don't know and it is frustrating."

I pause here and take a breath.

Reece stares at me. Her eyes are wide and blue and I can see empathy in them, even though it's dark.

"Don't feel sorry for me," I tell her. "Seriously."

"I don't," she answers. "I just sort of know how you feel."

I raise an eyebrow. "You've had amnesia?"

She laughs. "No, but I've had an identity crisis. When Dante and I first got together, I felt a little lost.

There I was, in love with Caberra's 'prince', but I was-
and still am- a farm girl from Kansas. I'm not from a
big, fancy family. I didn't even know how to act at
those black tie functions that Dante always has to
attend. If it weren't for you, I would've been totally
lost. But I eventually figured out that no matter what
situation I am in, I am always me. And that will
always include the fact that I am a Kansas farm girl,
born and bred. I will always eat steak sauce on my
steak and wear cowboy boots and I will always feel
more comfortable in worn out jeans than a ball gown.
But that's okay- because that's what makes me, *me*.
Your feisty spirit makes you, *you*. You will always be
witty and slightly rebellious. No matter how you
choose to act, or who you choose to be, you will
always be that sassy person that we all love."

"I do feel sassy," I tell her. "So that must be an
innate trait of mine."

"Yes," she smiles. "It is. Now, where did our
boys get to?"

Our boys?

I turn with her and search out the crowd. Quinn
is sitting next to Elena and they are deep in
conversation. He doesn't see me watching and that is
fine. Dante and Gavin are standing together on the
edge of the crowd. Gavin instantly catches my eye
and grins. And I am instantly reminded that his grin
is knee-weakening.

"He's got a gorgeous smile," I remark offhandedly to Reece.

"Yup," she agrees. "And he knows how to use it."

"Yup," I answer. Because he so, so does.

Dante motions to Reece to come join him and Gavin makes his way to me. He grins as he approaches, and I feel a little like a lion and its prey. Gavin doesn't look away the entire time he is walking. His dark eyes are fixed on me.

"So," he drawls as he stops next to me. "About that skinny-dipping thing? I honestly think you'll feel more like yourself if you start doing things that you used to do. I'm no doctor, but it makes sense. Don't you think?"

I smile. "Maybe," I say playfully and Gavin's eyes instantly fill with hope.

"Really?"

I shrug and decide to throw caution to the wind.

"Sure. Why not? Everyone else is back over that way and it's just you and me here. And apparently, we used to do this all the time. So, it's not like it's anything you haven't seen before."

I know as well as he does that we've never skinny-dipped. And he looks a bit startled now, but then he masks it and returns to his ultra-cocky self.

"Great," he tells me. "I'm glad you're up for it."

What he really means is, *Challenge Accepted.* He's not going to back down.

And neither am I.

I smile.

"Great," I say. I walk down to the water and start unbuttoning my shorts. The moonlight hits the water in ripples and makes it seem black, instead of the blue that I know it is. It's chilly and as I shrug out of my shirt, the breeze sends goose bumps forming down my arms. I rub them as I turn to Gavin.

"Why are you still dressed?" I ask. I know the answer is because he was watching me undress. But I pretend to not know that.

"Um, no reason," he says as he kicks off his shorts and unbuttons his shirt. He peels it off and then we're left staring at each other in our underwear. He's very muscular in a tall and slender way. Probably from swimming so much. I'm still wearing my bra and I suddenly feel exhilarated- although I don't know if it is from standing in front of Gavin in my panties or whether it is from all the rippling muscles on his abs.

It's one or the other, though.

"Come on," I tell him. I turn for the sea and strip off my underwear and bra at the water's edge, tossing it behind me into the sand. I dive into the water headfirst, allowing the cold water to rush over my naked skin.

I love this feeling. It's like I have no restrictions, no inhibitions and I'm totally free. I splash to the surface and turn to find Gavin right in front of me. His wet arms slide against mine and my breath freezes on my lips.

His gaze is dark.

His smile is wicked.

And so is mine.

"Come here," he tells me, pulling me to him. I slide against him, and every inch of us is naked and pressed together. *Every inch.*

My heart pounds as he kisses me. His hands are pressed into my back, pushing me closer into his chest. His fingers are warm while the rest of us is cold from the sea. The moon shines onto us, making our skin seem silver in the dark.

His lips slide away from mine, leaving my breath ragged and panty.

"Kiss me again," I instruct him, wrapping my arms around his neck.

"Done," he whispers. He lifts me up and I wrap my legs around his waist and he's pressing against me *there*. And I like it. I don't take the time to wonder what that makes me. Instead, I just kiss him again and again.

An image of Quinn pops into my head, but it is quickly overshadowed by an image of Quinn with Elena. Quinn made the choice, I didn't.

Gavin is right for me. I can feel it. And I'm pretty sure it's not the wine-coolers talking. I only had two.

He knows me. Really knows me. And that's got to be right for me in a time when I don't know myself.

His breath is ragged now, his heart pounding against my chest. His gaze is inky black in the night.

"Mia," he whispers. And he opens his mouth to say something else, but we are interrupted by flashing lights. White pops of light.

What the hell?

I'm disoriented for a minute, looking around to see where the light is coming from.

"Go," Gavin yells to me, pushing me toward the shore. And then he's gone. I can't even see where he went. I'm confused and then I see dark shadows moving on the shore with the white light.

Cameras.

Someone is taking our picture.

I'm astounded. Everything is happening in blurs and I don't even know what to do but sink into the water so that whoever it is can't see me naked. It's all so disorienting.

And then Quinn is striding toward me. His face is grim and set and he is taking off his shirt as he plows into the water. He doesn't even slow down.

When he reaches me, he stares down at me.

"Oh, the messes you get yourself into," he says quietly.

He scoops me out of the water and drapes his shirt around me. And then he carries me out of the sea. Men in suits have chased away the people with cameras. Dante's security detail, apparently. And I see Gavin on the beach, pulling his clothes on.

He starts to talk to me, but I interrupt, still ensconced in Quinn's arms.

"You left me!" I snapped. Gavin looks surprised.

"What would you have me do?" he asks, still clearly surprised. "They wanted our pictures. If our parents saw those pictures, we'd be in serious trouble."

"Who are *they*?" I ask, still aware that Quinn hasn't set me down. I can feel his strong arms encircling my naked body. His heat is scorching. Or that might be my temper. I can't tell.

"They are trying to get our pictures for their gossip sites," Gavin tells me. "They like to sneak out here when they think we might be having a party to catch unruly behavior on film."

And it dawns on him that these are things that I don't remember.

"Oh, god. Mia, I'm so sorry. I forgot that you wouldn't know what was going on. I'm sorry. I thought you would know to run for cover. I guess I did leave you."

He is genuinely apologetic. But that doesn't change the fact that he left me. And I'm fairly certain that when I was standing there like a deer in the headlights, they got many pictures of me. Naked.

OhLord.

"Can you take me home?" I ask Quinn. He nods.
"Of course."

He doesn't put me down, he just turns and walks over the sand dunes with me in his arms. I ignore Gavin's shouts from behind us as I look up at Quinn.

"You can put me down," I tell him. "I should get my clothes. They're on the beach."

As if on cue, Reece jogs up with my clothing in her arms.

"I've got her, Reecie," Quinn says before she can even speak. She nods.

"Okay. I just thought Mia might want to get dressed before you go back to the house."

Of course I do.

I can't imagine the look on my mom's face if I walk- or get carried- into Giliberti House as naked as the day I was born.

"Thank you, Reece," I sigh. "I guess some things don't change. I'm still getting myself into messes."

She shakes her head. "Gavin shouldn't have left you. He feels terrible though. I'll see you at the house. Here's Dante's keys. You can take his car. I'll find Dante and then meet you there. I'll have Gavin drop us off."

I nod. "Thank you- take your time."

She ducks back into the night and I see her blonde hair fading into the dark.

Quinn still hasn't put me down.

"There are bath houses up ahead," he tells me. "You can go inside and change without worrying about someone else taking a picture. I'll guard the door."

I am instantly relieved and indebted to him and impressed with his consideration. I am all of these things at once. And because there are so many things, I don't even know how to express them.

So I just nod and say, "Thanks."

Quinn grins down at me. "Sure thing, tiny tot."

He puts me down in the doorway of one of the little bath-houses and I very quickly pull on my clothes. When I walk back out, he is still alone, leaning against the wall of the building. He's so big, but he's got such a big heart, too.

"I will always remember you plunging into the water to save me," I tell him quietly. "Especially because you don't know how to swim."

He shakes his head.

"It wasn't that big of a deal," he tells me. "Seriously. The water was only chest deep. I saw you out there looking so confused and I knew I had to come get you. I had clothes on," he reminds me. "You didn't. That made it a little easier for me to walk in front of everyone. What possessed you to go skinny-dipping, anyway? You had to know that you guys are constantly watched for photo ops. If Dante's there, there's going to be photographers."

"I forgot," I tell him. "I didn't remember that."

And I feel deflated.

I feel the total opposite of how exhilarated I felt when I was in the water.

I still feel naked, though—just in a different way.

"Of course you didn't remember," Quinn says. "Someone should have reminded you." He's sympathetic now. And I hate that. But I don't say anything.

We ride to Giliberti House in silence. The irony that Quinn is driving Dante's car isn't lost on me. I can't help but constantly feel surprised at how well they get along now, when I know that they were on rocky terms at first.

"What's with you and Dante?" I ask as Quinn pulls into the Giliberti drive. He glances over at me.

"What do you mean?"

"You get along so well," I point out. "I figured that since you used to have a thing for Reece that you and Dante would butt heads."

Quinn laughs, a sound that is husky and rich in the night. Even his laugh has an American accent. I like it.

"Dante and I are fine," he tells me. "He didn't know what to think of me at first, but once he realized that Reece and I aren't a thing, he was fine. He's really easy to get along with."

"As are you," I tell him.

"Well, that's what I'm told," he tells me as he uncurls himself from behind the wheel. He comes around the car to open my door, like a gentleman. I love that, too.

He opens my door and helps me from the car and then walks me up the manicured sidewalk. He doesn't dwell on the fact that I was skinny-dipping and that he bailed me out. He'll never know how grateful I am. So I tell him.

He shakes his head again.

"It wasn't a problem," he tells me again. "You would've done the same for me."

And I would have. I really would have. That makes me happy. Maybe I really am a bad-ass.

"Why did you go to the party with Elena?" I ask him suddenly, before I lose my bad-ass nerve. He looks startled.

"Because she asked me. You didn't," he points out. "Why did you go with Gavin?"

I shake my head. "I didn't. I went with Reece and Dante."

"But you went skinny dipping with Gavin," Quinn reminds me.

"That was just me being impetuous," I tell him.

He stares down at me, his sandy blonde hair curling up at his neck.

"Well, maybe me going to the party with Elena was impetuous, too."

He's still staring at me, strong and silent in the dark. We're lingering in the doorway of the house, each of us hesitant to open the door and end this conversation. The whole mood feels like an open-ended sentence. And I want it to keep on going.

With Quinn.

"I don't know what I'm supposed to want," I admit to him. His eyes are like liquid chocolate as he assesses me. He seems pensive.

"Well, you're the only one who can figure that out," he finally tells me. And I know he is right.

"I'm just so confused," I murmur. "And I hate that."

"Well, tiny tot, don't stress so much about figuring it out," Quinn says. "When you're ready, the answer will be clear. You'll know what you want."

"I will?" I ask. I watch his lips as he speaks.

"You will," he assures me. "Trust me."

And as I picture his strong arms carrying me out of the sea while I was wrapped in his shirt, I know that I do.

I do trust him.

It's a good feeling.

Chapter Eighteen

I see a side to my mother this morning that I wish could have stayed locked in my lost memories. She's so furious about the pictures taken of me last night that she looks like she could just spit.

In fact, she accidentally does spit on my cheek as she hisses angry words. I wipe it away and patiently listen to her tirade.

And as she says something about me embarrassing her and my father, a memory slams into me.

You're an embarrassment.

I inhale sharply as a few more blurred and jagged memories come rushing back. I see a few faces and images and colors and it leaves me feeling nauseous and overwhelmed in a sea of emotion.

"We fought that day," I whisper. My knuckles are white as I fist them in my lap. My mother looks at me from my bedroom windows.

"What?" She is startled now.

"The day of the earthquake. You told me that I embarrassed you. We fought and I left. I was supposed to have been in my bedroom, but I sneaked away to go diving with Gavin."

"You remember?" she asks, her face pale. My mom is a small woman, and she looks severe today with her dark hair pulled into a tight chignon at her neck. I nod.

"I remember. That much, anyway. But it's something."

"You're right," she sighs. "It's something. Yes, we fought that day. You had your nose pierced. I wanted you to take it out so that you didn't embarrass your father. You refused. Then you left."

"And when I was in a coma, you took my nose ring out and colored my hair," I say calmly. She nods wordlessly.

"Why?" I ask. I feel limp. Even though I know what she did. I need an answer now. Am I really such an embarrassment to my parents that they would try to change me when I wasn't even conscious?

"Because we had to," she answers simply. "I thought that maybe everything could change. But I see now that it's not going to happen. You're going back to your old ways and there's nothing I can do about it."

"My old ways?" I raise an eyebrow and try to force my temper down. I feel my blood starting to boil and that's not a good sign. "Just because I see life differently than you do, doesn't make me wrong," I tell her. "If you and dad weren't so rigid about trying to force me into the mold of a person that I'm not, maybe you would see that."

"We're not trying to change you," my mother says. "We're just trying to change your behavior. You've got to realize that a mature person has to sometimes act in ways that they would rather not, simply because of their position in life. You have to act respectful and mature because of your father. It's just the way it is."

And all of a sudden, I see her point.

I don't know why, but it's like a revelation.

An epiphany.

Maybe Gavin was right and I can still be who I am, but I don't have to announce it to the world. Maybe I should fall into rank and do what is expected of me. At least part of the time. It wouldn't hurt me and it would make my life easier. I can do what I want on the side, but still do what my parents want. Then I wouldn't have to butt heads with them.

Butting heads with them takes so much energy.

"Okay," I say simply.

My mother stares at me.

"Okay?" she's incredulous.

I nod. "Okay. I'll try to be more considerate about daddy's image. I don't mean to be disrespectful."

My mother looks like she doesn't know whether to have a heart attack or whether she wants to cry and hug me.

So she just looks at me with her mouth open.

"I'm being serious," I tell her. "I'll try not to keep disappointing you."

And she flies into my arms with all the velocity of a raging bull.

A tiny raging bull.

"You're not a disappointment," she tells me as she strokes my hair. "I love you, Mia. Thank you for being so understanding. And for trying."

Holy cow. This was easy.

That's all I can think as my little bitty mother cries in my arms. I've made her so happy by simply not railing against her. I think Gavin was onto something.

"I'm not changing my hair though," I tell her. "But I won't get my nose re-pierced."

"Deal," my mother smiles. And it honestly makes me happy to see her happy. She's looked miserable for as long as I can remember. And probably way before that.

I can imagine that I was partially to blame.

"Fresh slate?" I ask her. I pull away and look at her face. Her eyes are as green as mine. And hers are wet.

She nods. "Fresh slate."

I hug her and am surprised by how good it feels…like a puzzle piece falling into place, somehow.

"Mia," she says slowly. "I was dreading telling you this, but maybe it won't be so bad now. There is a benefit tonight at the Old Palace. It is to raise money for people who have been the hardest hit by the earthquake. There will also be a few awards. Dimitri is going to give you and the other kids an award for helping with the clean-up. You should probably go."

I stare at her. Obviously, if I'm getting an award, I should go. But she seems so nervous about asking me.

"Holy cow. I must have been a monster," I mutter for the twentieth time this week. "Of course I'll go. I'm sure Dante and Reece will be there, too, right?"

Mom nods. "Yes. And Gavin and Quinn, too, among a few others."

"It's black tie?" I ask. She nods again, looking pained. She's dreading my reaction, still. I smile pleasantly.

"Okay. I'll need to go get a dress. But I look forward to it."

I don't look forward to it, but part of this new leaf that I've turned over means that I will not throw a fit. My mom looks infinitely relieved.

"Thank you, Mia," she tells me. She gives me another hug before she leaves. And I'm left alone in my bedroom.

I text Gavin.

Are u going to that benefit dinner tonight?

He answers, *Yep. U?*

I reply. *Yes. Sigh.*

Gavin comes back with, *Do u want a ride?*

I pause. I'm sure Dante and Reece will be going, so I can get a ride with them. Plus, if I'm honest, I have to admit that I'm still a little annoyed with Gavin for leaving me like he did last night.

Yes, I understand that he was flustered and forgot that I didn't know what was going on. But still. He left me.

And Quinn saved me.

That fact isn't lost on me.

I sigh loudly.

No, that's ok. I'll catch a ride with Reece and Dante- and I'll see u there.

Gavin take a little longer to answer this time, but finally comes back with, *Ok.* And it is accompanied by a frownie face.

I don't know why I just did that. I honestly don't. But for some reason, all I can think about today is Quinn. And how he looked as he plunged into the water to carry me out.

It makes my heart flutter.

Gavin makes me feel safe because he knows me. But Quinn makes me feel safe because I feel like he would never let anything happen to me. Not that I need a protector, because I don't. But it's still a nice feeling.

I duck out of my room to find Reece. I find her, along with Dante and Quinn, out on the porch sipping at fresh lemonade.

Reece looks up, concern apparent on her face.

"How are you doing?" she asks worriedly. I stare at her.

"What do you mean? I'm fine. Shouldn't I be?"

Now she's the one who is confused.

"The pictures," she says slowly. "And your mom was so upset. I bumped into her in the hall earlier."

"Oh," I answer. "She's okay now. I told her that I would try to stop being such a challenge for her. And I haven't seen the pictures. Should I see them?"

Reece looks uncertain and she glances at Dante.

"There's no reason you need to," he tells me. "It would just make you upset. It's our fault anyway. We should have reminded you that this happens to us sometimes."

"Particularly when Dante is around," Reece interjects.

"But this will blow over," Dante adds. "It always does. By this time next week, the gossip sites will be on to something else."

"You'd think that with all the real news with the earthquake, they'd report about that," Quinn mutters. "Not some teenagers at a party."

"I couldn't agree more," Dante answers. "But these websites are toxic and gossipy. They don't care about the real news. They just want things that will make people's tongues wag."

"Like Mia standing in the sea topless," Quinn rolls his eyes and I cringe at his words.

"Please tell me that they didn't get a shot of my girls," I plead. And by girls, of course I mean my boobs. Reece looks pained.

"Well, your girls are blurred out. But yes. It's clear that you're topless."

I cringe again. But there's nothing to be done. The damage is already done.

I square my shoulders.

"Okay. I'm putting it out of my mind," I announce. "So what if half of Caberra has seen my girls now—I've got to think about other things. Are you guys going to the benefit tonight at the Old Palace?"

They all nod. I turn to Reece. "I've got to go get a dress. Are you up for a short shopping excursion?"

"Of course," she answers. "I have to get a dress, too."

"Perfect," I smile. Dante is already handing over his car keys, the ever-perfect, ever-dutiful boyfriend. He pulls Reece to him and kisses her on the forehead, warning her to be careful on the curves. She smiles sweetly and tells him she will. And then she takes the curves too fast, anyway.

Twenty minutes later, we're shopping. Which is apparently one thing that hasn't changed about me. I will always love to shop.

* * * * * * * *

At 5:45 p.m., I'm standing in front of the mirror in my room. I look pretty hot, I have to admit. My hair is pulled into a chignon and I like the way the pink streaks show. My dress is black and soft and clings to my curves, falling just above my knee. My shoes are kick-ass three inch heels with cute straps that criss-cross part-way up my calves. I'm even wearing a strand of my mom's pearls. She was incredibly and amazingly happy about that. I wonder if I used to realize how little it would take to make her happy?

When it's time to go, Dante, Reece, Quinn and I pile into Dante's Maserati. Quinn and I are crammed into the backseat, which seems even smaller than it normally would because Quinn is so enormous. He takes up way more than half of the space. He just sprawled out and then laughed at me because he had pinned me against the seat. But if I'm honest, I will admit that I enjoy being crushed up against him.

He grins down at me, almost as if he can read my mind.

And I can see that he's enjoying the cramped quarters too. He stretches his arm out behind me and I curve into his shoulder.

And I like it.

I'm not gonna lie.

Dante drives quickly into town. Like, bat-out-of-hell quickly. And that is too quickly because I'm enjoying the heat from Quinn's body. Reece cringes as we cruise smoothly through the curves, but I don't blame her. It's where Dante had his car accident last summer.

I pause.

Did someone tell me that? Or was that a memory? I sigh. It's confusing sometimes. This amnesia thing really, really sucks. But it does seem like my memory is coming back in bits and pieces.

When we arrive, I can see Dante's security detail following us. They've been really good about trying to be inconspicuous. But in light of the assassination attempt last year, they are being very careful now. Particularly tonight, with all of these people swarming about. They aren't letting Dante out of their sight.

"I'm going to find my father," Dante says. "I'll meet up with you later?" I nod and Reece leaves with Dante. The security detail follows. Quinn and I are left alone.

Again.

I look at him.

Then I look at the lines waiting to get into the Old Palace's ballroom.

"I know a short cut," I tell him. And then we both stare at each other.

"You do?" Quinn asks, one eye-brow raised. "And you remember it?"

"I do," I confirm in a whisper. "I remember it."

The weird thing is that the memory just sort of appeared. It didn't spring out of nowhere with a big announcement. It's like it was just there, waiting for me to realize that I remember it.

So.

Strange.

I turn to Quinn. "Yes. I do remember," I repeat. "Follow me."

And we duck behind the lines and through the back hallways. Security lets us pass because they recognize me.

"Have a good evening, Miss Giannis," one of them says. He nods at me and I smile back. Quinn and I weave through the empty halls of the Old Palace.

"This building is amazing," Quinn tells me as we walk through a corridor with a gilded gold ceiling. The artwork hanging on the walls is authentic and expensive and there is exquisite art in every nook and cranny.

"It is," I agree. "It really is."

I wonder if I used to be blasé about it. After all, I was born and raised around this stuff. But I enjoy seeing the wonderment on Quinn's face as he takes it all in. I hope that I remain like he is right now — appreciative of the beautiful things in life, no matter how many times I see them.

Even if my memories come back.

The ballroom is decorated to the nines in silver and black decorations. I see Dante and Reece standing with Dimitri Giliberti toward the front of the room. He is in a military uniform with a sash, his typical formal dress.

And again, that is something that I suddenly remember as though it has been there all along.

Which it has.

I just didn't remember it until now.

I gulp.

My memories returning sporadically and without warning is a total mind bender. Seriously, I can barely wrap my mind around it.

So instead, I choose to ignore it.

"Would you like to dance?" I ask Quinn.

He stares at me hesitantly.

"What?" I cajole him. "The big brawny cowboy can ride a bull but can't dance?"

And now he rolls his eyes.

"Is that a challenge?"

"Does it seem like a challenge?" I ask innocently.

He sighs and grabs my hand. "Come on, tiny tot."

I smile victoriously as he leads me onto the polished dance floor. The crystal chandeliers sparkle above us and servers in black-tails and white gloves sail through the crowds with trays of champagne.

Quinn pulls me to him and we smoothly dance around the ball room floor. I look up at him.

"You're a surprise," I admit. "I figured you couldn't dance."

But then again, I figured he didn't own a pair of dress shoes, either. He's sexy as hell tonight in a tux and polished black loafers. What is it about a tuxedo that can make a boy go from handsome to movie star hot in two seconds flat? My heart flutters as Quinn grins at me crookedly.

And that's another thing. My heart has been doing a lot of fluttering lately, mostly over this crooked grin of his.

"I can most certainly dance," he tells me needlessly. And I say needlessly because he is demonstrating that fact right now. He *can* most certainly dance.

His arms feel really good wrapped around me. I almost sigh because this moment feels pretty perfect. The music is soft and soothing, Quinn is handsome and strong, and I am pressed against his strong chest. He smells delicious. I could go and on about why this moment rocks.

But unfortunately, it doesn't keep rocking.

Because as I look up, I see Gavin. He is standing casually with Dante and Dimitri, with a champagne glass dangling loosely from his fingers at his side. He is the picture of casual elegance—as if tuxedos were invented to be worn by him. But I'm not distracted by how handsome he is. Because the look on his face startles me.

He's upset.

With me.

That is apparent. I stare into his dark eyes and he looks pointedly away. And he stays looking away. He doesn't glance back at me. My stomach sinks like a rock.

"Is something wrong?" Quinn asks, as he stares down at me. I shake my head.

"No. I mean, yes. Maybe."

He stares at me again, his blonde eyebrows furrowed as he tries to figure me out.

"I'll be back, okay?"

He nods and releases my hand and I scamper through the crowd to get to Gavin. But when I reach the spot where he was, he isn't there anymore.

"Mia!" I hear Reece call to me. I gaze around and find her in the crowd and she is gesturing wildly toward something behind me. I turn and see Gavin disappearing into a hall. I'm after him like a shot.

I call out for him, but he doesn't stop.

So, I do the only thing I can think of to do.

I chase him.

I have no idea how he manages to stay so far ahead of me when I am running and he is walking. It's like something out of a bad horror movie. I just can't seem to catch up. I trip along in my heels until I finally get smart enough to take them off. And then I trip along after him barefoot.

But finally, he takes pity on me

As he reaches a door that opens to the outdoors, he turns. He is tall and lithe and handsome and he doesn't want to be with me. That much is apparent.

"What do you need, Mia?" And he sounds weary.

I'm confused.

"Why are you running from me?"

He smiles a small, tight smile.

"I'm not running. I'm walking. You're short enough that you have to run to keep up."

"Details," I sniff. "Why wouldn't you stop?"

"Because I don't want to talk to you right now," he answers simply. And that answer hurts. Because out of everyone in my life, Gavin has always been there for me.

"Why?" I ask softly.

"Because," he shrugs. "I don't want to right now."

"But why?" I demand. "You have to have a reason."

"Because I just realized something," he says. And his voice is cool and his eyes are a bit sad. It makes me apprehensive and scared to ask. But of course I ask anyway.

"What did you realize?"

Gavin is quiet as he stares at me. And the serious and slightly sad expression on his face scares me because I have never seen it before.

"What?" I blurt out. "What is wrong with you? What did you realize?"

Gavin sighs.

"I realized that you have never looked at me like you were looking at Quinn just now. And you probably never will."

And then he turns around and walks into the night.

And I am stunned.

Because I think he might be right.

Chapter Nineteen

I have no idea if he is right or wrong or what. But it doesn't matter. Because the look on his face was so horribly sad that I just want to wipe it away.

"Gavin, please — wait!"

I chase after him and tug on his arm. He doesn't even look at me as he stops by the pool. He looks achingly handsome in the light of the moon. The water moves next to us in aquamarine ripples and I stare into his face. I find that I want to reach up and stroke his cheek or wrap my arms around his shoulders or hug him tight. But I restrain myself.

"Gavin, I'm sorry. I told you... I don't know what I want. How can I possibly know that when I don't even know who I am?"

I can hear the desperation in my voice and so can he.

His face softens a bit in reaction.

"Gav, I told you this on the boat the other day. I *said* that I was afraid to pursue this because I never want to lose you. And you said that it wouldn't matter—that I would never lose you, no matter what."

Now his eyes are really soft as he looks down at me.

"So, you don't want to lose me... but you don't know that you want me, either?"

My heart hurts at his words.

Like, it literally hurts.

"I don't know what to say, Gavin," I tell him. "I know that I love you in some way. I know that you are sexy as hell and you make me laugh and you know me like no one else does. I know that I love being with you—I love laughing with you and swimming with you and kissing you. But something seems to be holding me back and I don't know what it is."

I'm crying now. I feel the tears streaking down my face and Gavin moves to wipe them away. I lean into his hand and he cups my cheek.

"Let me know when you figure it out," he says softly.

And then he leaves me by the pool.

Alone.

I am stunned.

Gavin, easy-going, always laughing, always ready Gavin, just left me alone because I hurt him.

And I definitely didn't mean to.

Yet I did.

And now my heart seriously hurts.

I sink to my knees by the water and cry. Anyone who ever thought I'm a bad ass should see me right now, because I cry until my lungs hurt. The ugly kind of cry, too. Not the pretty, delicate sniff-into-a-tissue cry. Oh, no. I'm crying the dreaded gut-wrenching, mascara-ruining ugly cry.

And I don't care.

I don't even care when I hear someone behind me.

"I need a minute," I call out, sniffing into my hand. I don't have a tissue, so I wipe my snotty nose on my hand. Gross, but necessary.

"Are you alright?"

Quinn's husky voice is quiet in the dark.

I freeze. I know I look like some sort of monster with black-rimmed swollen eyes and a runny nose. But worse than that, I don't want him to see me this way—sad and broken. Not when he thinks I'm some sort of bad-ass. And especially not when I'm crying because I don't know what my heart wants. How pathetic is that??

"I'm fine," I tell him without lifting my head.

There is more rustling behind me. And then I feel his hand on my back. It's warm and large and comforting.

"You don't seem fine," he says softly.

"I'm not," I admit limply. I look up now, knowing full well that he will see me in all of my raccoon-eyed glory. But he doesn't even flinch. He's just staring at me with the most concerned look.

"What's wrong?" he asks simply. "Can I help?"

I swallow.

"I don't know," I tell him. "Can you fix the holes in my memory so that I know what I want?"

Quinn stares at me. He's serious and calm and thoughtful as he tries to decide what to say. Finally, his lips move. I know this because I'm staring at them.

"No, I can't fix your memory," he tells me as he scoots closer to me. "But who cares? You don't need your memory to figure out what you want."

I snort, then remember too late that my nose is gunky and runny. I sound like a snotted up pig. I blush, but he doesn't seem to notice.

"You don't," he insists. "You know who you are even if you don't remember it."

"That's what Reece said," I mutter. "But it's easy to say when you're not the one who is clueless."

"Oh, I'm clueless," he nods. "Trust me. Or you can just ask Reece. She can tell you. I'm very, very clueless about many, many things."

I smile now, even through my snot.

"Why are you here?" I ask curiously. "How did you know I was out here?"

Quinn shakes his head. "It wasn't hard. When you ran out of the room chasing Gavin, I didn't think it was going to end well."

I'm still now.

The night is cool against my skin and my heart beats hard against my ribs. It's so quiet out here that I can almost hear it.

"You knew I was chasing Gavin? And you still came after me?"

Quinn nods slowly.

"How did you know that it wasn't going to end well?"

Quinn rocks back on his heels and he stares at the pool thoughtfully.

"I just knew. Gut instinct."

"So you came after me."

I'm stunned by this. What kind of boy would come after me when he knew that I was chasing another guy? Clearly, one who is self-confident. And Quinn is that. And clearly, a boy who is caring and kind. And Quinn is that, too.

But still.

Holy Whoa. How amazing is he?

"Thank you for not pressuring me," I tell him randomly. I feel so tired and drained. And I'm just so thankful for his presence. So I tell him that.

He smiles.

"You're welcome. And I'm not going to pressure you. Do I think you're cute as hell and twice as sexy? Yes. I do. Do I love your sassy-ass sense of humor? Yep. That too. But I'm going to wait until you realize that you like me, too. I might be clueless about many, many things, but even I know that I can't make someone like me. If someone likes you, they'll realize it. And then it will be worth the wait."

"You think I'm worth the wait?"

I'm whispering now. I don't know why because we're all alone in the moonlight. Quinn smiles his sexy lop-sided, knee-weakening grin.

"Yes. I do."

"You seem so confident that my mixed up head is going to decide that you're the one for me." I state this calmly as if this conversation wasn't insanely ridiculous. I'm sitting here with a gorgeous American cowboy discussing the fact that I don't know if I like him. Is this even happening? Ohmygosh.

"Oh, your mixed up head will definitely decide that," Quinn answers with a grin. Then he winks. "Because it's the right choice."

Then he grabs my hand, completely ignoring the fact that I've been wiping my nose with it. He pulls me to my feet.

"Will you dance with me?"

I look at him uncertainly.

"I don't really want to go back inside. I'm a mess. And I don't want to see Gavin right now."

"That's fine," Quinn assures me. "I meant right here. We can hear the music from here. And it's sexier to dance under the stars, anyway."

Quinn McKeyen can't get any sexier. I decide that in this instant. He pulls me to his tuxedoed chest and I rest my cheek against his satin lapel. His strong arms close around me and we sway together in the light of the moon.

My heart pounds.

He is so, so sexy.

And patient.

And strong.

And amazing.

I sigh.

He's got quite a long list of good traits.

I melt into him and let him hold me. And we dance, swaying together under the twinkling stars. We dance through the next several songs. Then we sit and chat by the pool. And then we dance some more.

And honestly, by the end of the evening, even in spite of the whole crumbling-into-a-sobbing-heap thing, I can say it's been the best benefit event I ever remember attending at the Old Palace.

I know that doesn't say a lot considering that my memory has holes in it.

But still.

****

I wake up to a knock on my bedroom door.

I growl and cover my head with my pillow. After not getting home until 2:00a.m, there is no way that I'm getting out of bed at 8:00.

Not.

Gonna.

Happen.

I bury my head deep under my pillows and squeeze my eyes shut.

But whoever it is won't give up. They knock again and again.

And then finally, they get tired of knocking.

My door opens.

And Quinn is standing there. He looks breathtakingly sexy and fills up my entire doorframe. He's wearing old jeans that fit him exactly right, his cowboy boots and a blue faded button up shirt. The shirt looks soft and worn and it hugs his chest.

I peer out from under my pillows to get a better look.

He grins at me.

"Why are you so early???" I groan, flipping onto my back and staring at him. "And so cheerful already? Plus, you're dressed and everything. Ugh."

He raises an eyebrow as he approaches the bed. I only just now notice that he's carrying two cups.

"Would you prefer that I wasn't dressed?" he asks innocently. He holds out a cup. "I come bearing gifts. Coffee with one shot of espresso plus enough cream and sugar to make cake batter."

I stare at him now as I sit up.

"How did you know how I like my coffee? Stalk much?"

Quinn laughs and I decide that I might want to marry his laugh. It's just that sexy.

"I don't stalk you, tiny tot. I don't have to. I know you'll come to me someday. I asked Marietta how you take your coffee. And then she made it. So if it sucks, don't blame me."

I smile and roll my eyes.

Marietta might have made it, but Quinn brought it to me. And that's pretty dang sweet. But I don't say that.

Instead, I take a sip of the nectar of the gods and stare at him over the cup.

"So, what's the occasion? Why have you come bearing gifts?"

Quinn perches himself on the edge of my bed. And no, the fact doesn't escape me that now Quinn is technically in my bed. With me. And I'm half naked.

My heart flutters again.

Down girl, I silently tell it. Then I return my attention to Quinn, waiting for an answer.

"I want to continue with your riding lessons. And I figured you'd need some coffee to wake up."

I'm already shaking my head.

"Oh, no. I don't get up this early. The old me didn't and the new me doesn't either. And neither one of us is getting up this early to go riding on a gigantic demon. Nope. Not gonna happen."

I am up and dressed five minutes later.

Hey, don't judge.

Quinn can be pretty compelling while sitting on the side of my bed smiling at me.

Okay, fine.

I'm weak. Weak, weak, weak. Quinn's cocky grin does that to me.

But I admit it, so that's something, right?

Right before I duck out the door to meet Quinn outdoors, I text Gavin.

I'm really sorry about last night. I hope you can forgive me. I hate that you're upset.

There's no immediate answer. And I leave my phone in my room.

Quinn is already waiting for me outside. And now he's wearing his cowboy hat which only makes him even sexier.

"Hey tiny tot," he greets me. "I have something for you."

And he hands me a pale pink cowboy hat.

No. Lie.

I laugh as I take it and shove it onto my head.

"Where in Caberra did you find a cowboy hat?"

He grins. "There's a woman in town who makes straw hats. I showed her mine and asked her to make a smaller one for you. In pink. She did a good job."

I feel sassy now in my pink hat. I find myself wishing that I had a pair of shorts and boots on like Reece always wears.

"Thank you," I tell him. "I love it. I feel so American now."

He chuckles. "Well, surely you know that all Americans aren't cowboys. In fact, *most* Americans aren't even cowboys. Just some of us. The awesome ones."

I smile up at him. "Okay, Awesome One, tell me more about America."

So, as he saddles up Titan, he does. I stay a safe distance away from Titan's enormous stamping foot, but still close enough to listen. And obviously, close enough to watch Quinn's muscles flex as he lifts the saddle.

Because that's important.

"We like good barbeque, football and Sunday naps. We like pep rallies and college ball teams and ice cream. And French fries. We like animals and some girls even carry little dogs around in purses. But I could never see you doing that. We like working hard to be the best we can be. We love Disney World, no matter how old we are. And we love riding in Jeeps with the tops down. We love target shooting. We love firecrackers and the Fourth of July. We love going to the lake on a summer day, especially in a speed boat."

He looks at me as he adjusts Titan's bridle. "Is that enough or do you want to know more?"

I smile at him.

"Every American likes those things or just you? Because I honestly don't see Reece target shooting."

Quinn smirks. "Well, *most* Americans probably love those things. *I* certainly do."

"I've never been to America," I tell him. "So, I have no way of knowing if you're exaggerating. I'd planned on coming to visit Reece at some point, but now she's here."

"Well," he tells me. "You'll just have to come visit me instead. I mean, you need to know if I'm telling you the truth, right?"

And he literally stops what he is doing and stares into my eyes. His are warm and brown and chocolately. And I feel flustered for a second. Lost. And then he smiles.

"Deal?"

I swallow and nod.

"Deal."

He's satisfied with that. And he boosts me onto Titan. And I forget for a second that I am terrified because Quinn is swinging up behind me. I twist around to look at him.

"Tandem horseback riding?"

"I thought you could use a break today from things that stress you. So we're going to have a relaxing ride today. You just sit back and let me do the work."

So I do.

I settle back against him, enjoying the way his chest is hard and strong. I seem to melt into it and we fit just right. His arms curve around me and I am encompassed there. And I really like being here in this spot. He makes me feel safe and sound and warm. I love the way his chest feels as he talks, and I love the way his voice is smooth, yet husky.

And then I am faced with a big realization.

I love quite a few things about him.

It's a bit scary.

But then I'm distracted by the stubble on his chin as he dips his head to talk to me. So I grin up at him and before I even know what I'm doing, I'm twisting around to kiss him.

I am as surprised by this as he is, but he recovers first.

He wraps an arm around me, pulling me close. His tongue delves into my mouth, his breath hot. When he finally pulls away, I feel like panting again.

There should be a law against being as sexy as Quinn McKeyen.

"What was that for?" he asks softly. His chocolate brown eyes are glued to mine.

"I don't know," I tell him honestly. "I just wanted to."

"That's as good a reason as any," he answers. "Maybe your heart is starting to give you answers."

And maybe he's right. But I don't say that.

Instead, I lean against him again. And I enjoy the ride. Titan walks smoothly, his large muscles contracting beneath us. The sun feels so good on my face that I almost fall asleep. I'm still tired from my late night. We ride through the entire property, weaving amongst the olive trees and down by a natural creek that runs on the property. We take a few minutes there to stretch and let Titan drink. Then we ride more.

Finally, several hours later, Quinn guides Titan back toward the house and I close my eyes, basking in the sun like a contented cat. I am seriously almost asleep when Titan stops.

I open my eyes. And I get the surprise of my life. And not a good surprise, either.

Gavin is here.

He's standing next to the corral, apparently waiting for me, and he isn't happy to see me riding with Quinn.

Efffff.

Chapter Twenty

"Hi Gavin," I call out.

He doesn't answer.

Efffffffff.

"Will you be alright?" Quinn asks me quietly.

"Of course," I tell him. "It's fine." He nods and helps me down from Titan, then heads to the stable.

I walk straight to Gavin. And Gavin is not happy. At all.

"What are you doing, Mia?" he asks. And there are thunderclouds on his face. I've never seen him look quite so mad. Actually, I don't know that I've ever seen Gavin mad at all. I gulp.

"I went for a ride."

"Yes, I see that. With Quinn. *Literally*, with Quinn. You were basically on his lap."

Is he jealous? Holy cow.

"Well, to be fair, there's only one horse and I don't really know how to ride yet. So, Quinn was kind enough to take me for a ride."

Gavin scoffs. "Oh yeah. He's being kind. There's nothing in it for him."

And now he's being facetious. And definitely jealous. That's not like him.

"You weren't answering your phone," he points out.

"That's because it's in the house," I tell him. "I texted you this morning and you ignored me. So I just left it inside."

"Convenient," Gavin says wryly.

"What is wrong with you?" I demand. "You wouldn't even talk to me last night. And here you are pissed off that I went for a ride with Quinn."

As I speak, I glance toward the stables to see if Quinn has emerged, but he hasn't. He must still be taking care of Titan. I decide that's best, considering how agitated Gavin is.

"What is wrong with me is that ever since your accident and I saw that things could change between us, in a good way, I've felt better than I have in a long time," Gavin tells me. "You and I together is a very good thing. We know each other. We would fit so easily into each other's lives. And all of a sudden, you're too nervous to try and pursue it. And you've never been nervous a day in your life. I don't understand it. And now you've taken up with Quinn. And I can't figure you out."

I stare at him.

"Do you want to be with me?" I ask. "Or do you want to be with the idea of me… because we would 'fit so easily into each other lives?"

Gavin rolls his eyes. "Don't twist my words, Mi," he tells me. "You know what I mean."

"I *don't* know what you mean," I answer. "And I haven't 'taken up with Quinn'. I went for a ride with him. We didn't run away and get married."

Gavin is angry now. His tan cheeks are flushed. I can see that he's trying to rein it in and I don't understand it. I don't know where his anger is coming from.

"Mia, I'm worried about you. And your decisions. Quinn isn't like us. He's not from here. And I like him, I do. So it's not that. But you don't realize right now, because you're not yourself… but you can't just got trotting off with someone you barely know. Not in your position. I hate to say this, but you don't have the best track record with guys. You thought you knew Vincent Dranias too, but look how that turned out. Dimitri, Dante and Elena could have all been killed."

I suck in a breath and Gavin goes still.

And I go still. And my blood turns cold.

"I'm sorry, Mia," Gavin says quickly. "I crossed the line. I didn't mean it."

"But you did," I answer slowly. "You did mean it. You don't think I can think for myself. And you think that the assassination attempt was my fault."

He looks pained now.

As he should.

I jut my chin out.

"Mia, that's not what I meant. That wasn't your fault at all. It was Nate's fault. And if you hadn't fallen for Vincent, they would have just found another way into our circle. I just meant that you aren't yourself. Now isn't a good time for you to make rash decisions."

"But I haven't made any decisions," I point out. "None. And I think that's really why you are mad. You thought I would just fall into your arms and that would be that."

"Well, that would certainly have made things easier," he says wryly. "But you're far too stubborn for that."

"No, I'm not," I insist.

"Yes, you are," he nods. But at least he's smiling now.

And then suddenly….something about his smile, or the light hitting his face, or the way he's looking at me, or something that I can't put my finger on… *something* triggers my messed up mind.

There is a weird sort of flicker in my thoughts, like a blur.

Everything sort of swirls together in a huge chaotic mess of colors and lights and words.

And then everything comes crashing down.

I remember everything.

Everything.

I remember diving with Gavin, I remember being friends with him since preschool. I remember meeting Reece for the first time. I remember lashing out at my parents. I remember all of the black gothic clothing I wore. I remember my car. I remember countless charity events at the Old Palace. I remember going to school.

I remember everything.

"I remember," I murmur.

And I sink to my knees because the suddenness of it, the enormity of it, is overwhelming. I actually feel nauseas.

"You remember?" Gavin asks and he is concerned now as he bends next to me. "How? Are you alright?"

I don't know. I feel like throwing up. And I don't know why.

I rock back and forth on my heels as I focus on my thoughts, on all of the faces in my thoughts. Of Elena- and how she is the world's biggest bitch and how could I forget that? I remember Reecie and Dante and Nate and Vincent.

Oh My God. Vincent. I remember Vincent. And Gavin is right. I used very poor judgment with Vince. But how in the world could I have known better? He was hiding who he was from me. That wasn't my fault.

And I remember Gavin.

I stare at him now. At his handsome face and his white smile. But now, all of a sudden, I don't see him as a heart-stoppingly sexy guy. I see him as my good friend. That is immediate and apparent. He is and always will be my friend. It's like my heart turned a complete one-eighty. I can't help how I feel. And just like I was afraid of, my memories have changed everything.

Gavin stares back.

"Do you remember me?" he asks quietly.

I nod.

And his expression falls.

"Hey," Quinn yells from the stable door. "Mia! Are you okay?"

My head snaps up and my eyes meet his.

And he rushes toward me.

But Gavin stands up and all of a sudden, his frustration with the situation has a target. A target who doesn't deserve it, but is a target nonetheless.

Quinn.

Gavin rushes at him with an aggression that I've never seen in him. Quinn startles as he realizes what is going on and then he does the only thing he can do.

He defends himself. He braces himself for impact.

Gavin plows into him and slams him to the ground.

Quinn's head whips back and I hear it crash into the ground with a sickening thud. My stomach clenches at the sound. He hits hard. And then Gavin punches him. Hard. I can hear his knuckles smash into Quinn's cheek.

And then Quinn roars like a lion.

He throws Gavin off, and Gavin tries to come back for more. Quinn is able to hold him at bay.

"You don't want to do that," Quinn says. I think he's pretty calm, considering the situation. His lip is split and it is bleeding. And I know he's holding back. He's not thrashing Gavin the way he could.

"You don't know what I want," Gavin snaps.

"Oh, I do know," Quinn says. "And I'm sorry that you can't have her."

And then Gavin punches at him again. But this time, Quinn catches his fist in his large hand and squeezes, forcing Gavin away. But Gavin won't give up. He brings his knee up and slams it into Quinn's gut. I hear the air whoosh out.

And suddenly, Quinn has had enough.

He punches Gavin. Hard. In the face.

Gavin flies backward into the dirt. And he lays there, still.

I find my wits now and rush to him.

"Are you alright?" I shake his shoulder. He's dazed, but he opens his eyes. "Gavin, are you okay?"

I am panicked now. Blood seems to be everywhere. His hand is bleeding, his nose. I twist around and see that Quinn's face is streaming blood, too.

This can't be happening.

OhMyGod.

"Gavin?" I say, and my voice is shaky. "Can you hear me?"

He actually smiles for a second, but then he turns serious.

"Of course I can hear you. I'm not deaf."

He pushes me off of him and he gets to his feet.

He stares down at me.

"This isn't the right decision, Mia," he tells me. And then he walks away before I can even answer.

Quinn takes a step and offers me his hand.

"Are you okay?" he asks me. And I have to laugh at that. He's got blood streaming everywhere and he's asking me if I'm okay.

"I'm fine," I tell him. "How about you?"

He touches his cheek gingerly and I see that his hand is swollen already. I start to grab it, but restrain myself. I don't want to cause him more pain.

"Oh my god, I think your hand might be broken," I tell him worriedly. He nods.

"I'm pretty sure it is. Don't worry about it. It won't be the first time."

I stare at him.

"Do you get in fights often?"

He grins his crooked grin.

"Did I forget to mention that's one of the things Americans like to do?"

"You like to get into fights?" I'm incredulous. He smiles, then shakes his head.

"I'm kidding. But I do live in a small rural town. There's not much to do, so the majority of us have gotten into a fight or two. What I really meant was that I've broken a few bones playing football. It's okay. I'll heal."

"You need ice," I tell him as I grab his arm and spin him toward the house. I'm not sure how I know this, but it seems logical.

He stops.

"Are you okay?" he asks me quietly. "I heard you. Your memories are back. Do you need to go see a doctor, or…"

I stare at him in utter disbelief. He's dripping blood and he's worried that I'm the one who needs a doctor? I mention the ridiculousness of this to him and he smiles.

"I'm sorry. I don't have any experience with this whole amnesia thing. It just makes sense that you would need to see your doctor."

I shrug. "Maybe I do, but not as much as you do right now."

"I'm fine," he insists. And as he does, he wipes the blood from his lip. I shake my head.

"You aren't fine," I tell him.

He ignores that. "What was that even about?" he asks. "What set Gavin off like that?"

I pause. I don't have a great answer.

"I... um. I think that Gavin has tried a very long time to be everything that everyone needs—the perfect son, the perfect friend. He tries very hard to be laid back and easy going. And when I lost my memory, I think he saw an opportunity to be part of a relationship with someone who understands what it is like to be with someone like him--- we have the same social pressures. But tonight, he knew that wasn't going to happen. And I think that everything just sort of exploded for him. All of his pent up frustrations and whatnot. It didn't have anything to do with you. Don't take it personally, although I know that's hard."

Quinn nods, but before he can say anything, I hear voices.

I turn to find Dante and Reece running toward us.

"What happened?" Reece breathes as she skids to a stop next to us. "Oh my gosh, Quinn! What the hell? We saw Gavin leave and he was bloody. And you're bloody...." She trails off and stares. "Holy monkeys. You got into a fight."

"Are you alright?" Dante asks quietly. He's glancing over Quinn, at his split lip and swollen hand. I see now that Quinn's eye is a bit swollen too. I gulp.

Quinn nods. "I'm fine, guys. I've had worse than this after a game. Trust me."

Reece narrows her eyes. "What were you fighting about?" And then she looks at me. I exhale shakily. I'm still feeling nauseas.

"I remember everything," I tell her. "Gavin was upset because I was riding Titan with Quinn and for some reason, something triggered my memories and they all came back. And now I think I'm going to throw up."

And I do. I barely have time to turn away before I am dropping to my knees and puking my guts up.

I hear movement behind me and Reece holding my hair back. She pats my back. But it's Quinn's voice that murmurs to me that it's going to be okay.

I glance back and find that it is Quinn comforting me. Reece is standing a short distance away, looking for all the world like she wants to shove him out of the way and kneel next to me, but she doesn't. She lets Quinn do it.

Another wave of nausea floods through me and I throw up again. And then I'm okay. I sit still for a second, then I wipe my mouth and turn around.

I try to stand up, but my knees are weak. I feel shaky.

And I grab onto Quinn's strong arm.

Instead of helping me up, he just scoops me into his arms.

He carries me the entire way to the house, up the stairs, down the hall and into my bedroom. My mother's face is shocked as we pass her in the foyer, and she follows behind with Reece and Dante.

Quinn sets me on the bed.

"You're going to be fine," he tells me. And I'm not sure if he is comforting me or giving me a directive. But I nod. Either way, he's right.

I'll be fine.

I know that now.

Chapter Twenty One

Reece sits with me for the entire first twenty-four hours. My mother takes the doctor's order to rest to heart and refuses to let me leave my bed, so my friends come to me. Dante comes to play chess. Quinn comes to chat and bring me coffee. Reece is always here. We look at fashion magazines, do our nails and she flat-irons my hair.

Gavin doesn't come.

I try not to let this hurt. Reece texted him and told him that I'm alright, that my memories have all returned. She relayed what the doctor told us… that my brain has now made a full recovery. She joked with him that I'm still not right in the head, but I'm as right as I ever was.

He replied that he's glad I'm okay.

That was it.

And that really hurts.

But I have to try and look at it from his point of view. And when I do that, I feel really sad. Because he was right. It would have been very convenient if we'd have gotten together. And I think his feelings really did change toward me after the accident. I think that New Mia was exciting for him. It was like meeting someone new, yet someone who was familiar and safe. Just like I felt about him.

Felt.

Past tense.

Because those fluttery feelings that I had for both Quinn and Gavin are gone. And they are solely focused on Quinn alone now. Of that, I am certain.

Everything Quinn does sends my heart into a tail spin. My hormones burst into flame whenever he is near. My heart has clearly decided. But I haven't told Quinn yet. I'm trying not to be impetuous. New Mia has turned over a new leaf.

"So," Reece says as she hands me a hot pink shirt. "New Mia is sticking around?"

She is trying to hide her surprise, I can tell. She was amazed when I told her that I don't need to go shopping to replace my new wardrobe with another new wardrobe consisting solely of black.

I nod. "New Mia is here to stay, with bits of Old Mia thrown in. Old Mia was trying too hard to prove a few points and all she did was piss people off. New Mia has had some revelations."

Reece raises a blonde eyebrow. "Like?"

"Like it's okay to be agreeable. It's okay to do things that you don't really want to do—if those things are helping out people you love. I have to understand that my dad's job is important and that people watch me. Gavin was right about that—I need to suck it up and do my part. But that doesn't mean that I can't do it in my own way. I won't put my nose-ring back in, but I'm leaving my hair. It's not hurting anything. I'm compromising on the clothes. I don't feel the need to wear black, but I'm not wearing beige. Ugh."

Reece smiles. "Hot pink is a compromise? And fingerless gloves?"

I nod. "Yes. I believe those are fair compromises."

Reece laughs. "I like New Mia. She's still pretty kick-ass, too." But then she gets serious. "What about Quinn?"

I stare at her. "I like him," I tell her quietly. "I really like him."

She nods. "I know. I can tell. And he likes you too. So what are you going to do about it?"

I smile. "Well, there's one thing that New Mia and Old Mia have in common."

"And what's that?" Reece asks.

"We both work hard to get what we want."

Reece laughs at that and I laugh with her.

"Am I going to have to listen to you refer to yourself in the third person now for all of eternity?" she asks with a grin.

"Possibly," I tell her. "I sort of like it. It makes me feel like the Queen of England."

Reece rolls her eyes and hands me a pair of jeans.

"Well, come on, your highness. Get dressed."

I pull my pants on and we wind our way down the stairs and into the kitchen. I am surprised to find my mother there, along with Dante. She's as casual as can be about eating in the kitchen.

What the hell?

"Mom?" I look at her in surprise. She's sitting with Dante, nibbling at a croissant and sipping a cup of coffee.

She smiles at me and she honestly looks happy.

My mother.

Happy.

It's a crazy concept, I know.

But it seems to be true.

"Don't look so surprised," she tells me. "I'm not too old to change, you know. I thought about it a lot last night when I was supposed to be sleeping. You might have been right all along. I was too rigid and set in my ways. Some might even say that I was being a witch." She pauses here, presumably waiting to have someone refute that. No one does. She sighs. "I'm probably partially to blame for you rebelling so hard. So, I've decided to take a page from your playbook and reassess my life. Changes will be made."

I'm stunned.

This is amazing.

I gulp, then nod.

"Thank you," I tell her. "I don't know what to say."

"There's nothing to say," she tells me. "Everything will be alright, Mia."

And once again, I believe that to be true. Everything really will be okay.

"Have you seen Quinn?" I ask. My mother nods.

"He was here for breakfast. I think he went outside."

I chat for a moment longer before I go outside to find him. Reece stays inside to talk with my mom and wait for Dante.

It doesn't take me long to find Quinn. I just head down to the stables and there he is. He is truly in his element with that horse. That is for sure. I walk up to the fence and call out a good morning. He turns and I inhale sharply. It looks like a truck has hit his face.

"Holy cow," I breathe. "Your face."

He smiles. "Gee, thanks," he says. "Just the kind of reaction I was looking for."

He's joking and I smile.

"Does it hurt?" I ask hesitantly. He rolls the eye that isn't swollen.

"It doesn't feel wonderful. But I'm okay," he assures me.

I gaze at him, at his handsome, sexy face that is now swollen and distorted. He smiles. Or I think he does. With his cheek swollen like that, it's hard to tell. And then he rolls his eye. The un-swollen one.

"Way to make me feel unselfconscious, tiny tot," he tells me wryly.

I wince. "I'm sorry. It just looks painful. I'm so sorry that this happened to you. It's my fault. That's what I was coming to say to you. To apologize, I mean."

He stares at me like I've suddenly grown two heads.

"The last I knew, Gavin was the one who attacked me," he tells me. "Not you. So don't feel guilty at all, Mia. It's not your fault."

"If I hadn't been so confused, Gavin wouldn't have felt led on and this entire thing wouldn't have happened," I tell him sadly. "It *is* my fault."

He shakes his head. "Well, we'll have to agree to disagree. But on the off chance that you're right and this *is* your fault, there's something you can do to make it up to me."

He pauses here and grins. Or I think he does. It's hard to say at this point with all that swelling. I choose to believe it is a grin and so I grin back.

"And what would that be?" I ask.

"You can finally teach me to swim," he answers. "If I'm here in Caberra, surrounded by the sea, I think it's something I should know, don't you?"

I smile and start to nod.

Unfortunately, I don't have time to agree because a car rolls to a stop next to the stable. A police car from Valese. I'm startled as two officers climb out and head over to us. My heart pounds, although I don't know why. We haven't done anything wrong.

"Quinn McKeyen?" one calls out in English.

Quinn nods. "Yes, that's me." He's unconcerned because he knows that he hasn't broken the law.

The officer pulls out a pair of handcuffs. "You're under arrest for the assault of Gavin Ariastasis. Son, you picked the wrong boy to pick a fight with. Don't you know who his father is?"

The officer snaps on the cuffs and I am dismayed and astounded. So much so that I hear a roaring in my ears. I'm so flabbergasted that it takes a minute for me to come to my senses and say anything.

"Don't you know whose property this is?" I demand as I chase after them. "This is Dimitri Giliberti's property, as I'm sure you know. I don't think he'll like finding out that you've just arrested his house guest."

The officer levels a gaze at me.

"Miss, there's one thing about our prime minister. He's always fair. If his own son broke the law, he wouldn't step in to pull any strings. He believes that the law is the same for everyone."

I gulp because I know he's right. Dimitri is known for that.

"But Quinn was only protecting himself," I attempt. "I was there. I saw it. It was self-defense. Gavin started it. And I can't believe Gavin would press charges."

The other officer interrupts. "It wasn't Gavin who came down to the police station today. It was his father. You'll have to take it up with him."

Eff.

Gavin's father does have a temper. No one likes to cross him. In fact, it's probably one of the reasons why Gavin has always chosen to be so laid back. He wants to be the opposite of his high-strung father.

Eff again.

"Quinn, don't worry," I call to him as they put him in the car. "I'm going to get Dante. And my dad, too."

Then it occurs to me. My dad is every bit as important as Gavin's. So I call out to the officers.

"Do you know who *my* dad is? I'll have him down at the station before you can even blink. Maybe he'll even meet you there."

Quinn is shaking his head but I can't hear what he is saying because the door is closed now. I'm guessing he's telling me not to drag my father into it. But holy hell. This entire mess is my fault and I've never asked my dad for any favors. I think it's about time to start.

I am watching limply as the police car rolls back out when Reece comes to find me.

"Is that what I think it was?" she asks curiously.

I nod miserably. "Yes. And Quinn's in the backseat."

"What?" She is as appalled as me. I tug at her hand.

"Come on. We have work to do."

****

To my mother's credit, she drops what she is doing to drive me to see my father. I explain the entire situation to her on the way and she actually seems sympathetic. I have no idea what has come over her, but I hope it never goes away.

And while I am going to see my father, Dante is going to see his. We both tried to call Gavin, but he's not picking up his phone. I can't imagine what is going through his head, other than he probably doesn't want to go against his father.

But still.

If ever there was a time for him take a stand, now is the time.

My father is surprised when my mom and I burst into his large office in the Old Palace. He is even more surprised after I tell him why.

"Quinn? The nice boy who is Dimitri's exchange student?" he asks. I nod.

"Yes. And he is a nice boy. What happened wasn't his fault. And I'm afraid that if these charges go through, he'll have to go back to America. And that's not fair."

My father studies me. "And you don't want him to leave."

It's an observation, not a question. I flush, but I don't deny it.

"No, sir. I don't."

I even call him sir.

He thinks about this and stares out this window. I've never asked him for any kind of favor before. I've never, ever played on his status or importance. Not even one time. And I think he realizes that because he finally sighs.

"Okay, Mia. I'll talk to Dimitri. But I'll also speak with Gavin's father. Surely, if it is as you are saying and Gavin started it, he will see reason."

But even my father doesn't sound hopeful about that one. Gavin's father isn't known for his reason.

"The best thing you can do is go wait at the police station. I'm sure he will be released on bail today because this is his first offense, correct?"

I nod. "I think so. I'm sure it is."

My father nods. "Good. Go wait at the police station. Your mother can bail him out."

My mother looks a bit surprised by daddy's willingness to help, but she seems satisfied with it.

I'm overwhelmed by my parents' behavior today and I rush at my dad and hug him.

"Thank you, daddy," I whisper. "Thank you so much."

I feel a tear coming out of my eye and I wipe it away. My father stares at me in surprise. I don't usually cry in front of him. Or hug him. Or show him any emotion at all other than anger.

I smile.

"I really appreciate this, daddy."

I leave with my mom and she drives me to the police station, a place that neither of us have ever been. I can't even believe that my mother, the woman who just recently wouldn't bring herself to eat in a kitchen, is now going to walk into a police station to post bail. It's incredible. And a little funny.

I can't help but laugh about it, and so when my mom asks what I'm laughing about, I tell her and she laughs too.

"Mia, I know that I've been a stuck up snob. It's easy to get sucked into that kind of thing. And I'll probably always be a bit of a one. You can't completely change a person. But I'll try to be a nicer snob. How about that?"

I feel like crying again.

But I don't.

Instead, I smile and nod and my mother and I square our shoulders and disappear into the Community Police Station of Valese.

There's someone I have to save.

Chapter Twenty Two

"I told you," Quinn tells me yet again. "I'm fine, Mia. Don't stress about this. It's going to be fine."

The person who I saved turned out to be quite calm when we rescued him.

When he came walking out of the back hall of the police department, I thought my knees were going to give out. His eyes met mine and I knew that I would do anything I possibly could to keep him out of trouble and in Caberra.

With me.

It was an intense moment.

And now we're standing in the Great Room at Giliberti House. Well, scratch that. We're not standing. I'm pacing around like a mad woman, while Dante, Reece, Quinn and my mother are all sitting. Calmly. Like rational adults.

I'm the only one acting like a lunatic.

I recently had a head injury, though, so I have an excuse.

"It's not fine," I tell him. Then I grit my teeth. I've been gritting my teeth so much that I'm giving myself a headache. "We had to bail you out of jail. If we don't get this straightened out, they'll send you home—for something that wasn't even your fault."

"Mia," my mom interjects. "There is no use pacing around here and worrying. We have attorneys looking at this and your father is attempting to speak with Stefan Ariastasis. Perhaps he will see reason and this will just fade away."

"Fat chance," I mutter. "Gavin's dad isn't reasonable."

"Well, perhaps he will be this time," my mother insists. "I want you to go outside and take a walk. You should get some fresh air. You need a distraction."

"Speaking of distractions," Dante interjects. "My father is christening our new yacht today. It's sort of sentimental, actually, since we're replacing the boat we could have been killed on with a new one. Plus, our old yacht was named after my mother. And our new one is named for Reece."

This surprises me, because I didn't know anything about this. But then, I've been wrapped up in my own problems lately. Suddenly, I feel like a terrible friend.

"I didn't know any of this, D," I tell him. "I'm so sorry. What are you naming it?"

Dante grins, a brilliantly white smile that is full of pure adoration as he stares at Reece.

"The Sunflower."

I have to smile. Kansas, Reece's native state in America, is apparently filled with sunflowers. It's why Dante is always calling her his sunflower. And I get a huge lump in my throat because this is the sweetest thing on the planet.

"That is so sweet," I tell him. I don't know why my eyes feel like tearing up. I've been so emotional lately. So again, I blame it on my injury. That injury comes in sort of handy.

"Isn't it?" Reece asks happily. "I couldn't believe it when he told me."

I can believe it. Dante adores her. And I'm suddenly once again envious of their relationship. I feel ashamed of that envy though. If anyone deserves it, it's them.

"So, we're christening it today," Dante continues. "And I know it seems like a bad time, but it might be a good distraction for you to come. We're having a little party on the boat afterward for close friends and it might be a good opportunity to talk with Stefan."

I stare at him. "That's an excellent idea," I tell him. I glance at Quinn. "Want to go?"

He shrugs and smiles. "Sure. Apparently, I've never met a party that I didn't like."

He's so casual and cool and collected about everything that it makes my heart constrict. If it were me, I'd be flying off the handle and freaking out. But he's not. He's as calm as can be. We're like yin and yang. Perfect opposites.

"How about we go for that walk now?" Quinn asks me quietly.

"Sure," I tell him.

We leave everyone else in the Great Room as we head out the back doors into the fragrant gardens.

"Your concern for me is sweet," he tells me as we walk down the picturesque winding stone path. I glance at him.

"Of course I'm concerned for you. I can't believe this is happening. You can't go home right now. You just…can't."

He stops. We're hidden behind flower vines now, a good distance from the house beneath our own little canopy of white flowers. I gulp a big mouthful of the scented air.

"Is there a reason why not?" he asks huskily. "Is there a reason why you want me to stay?"

I am frozen as I look into his brown eyes.

There are hundreds of reasons. I can't even begin to list them.

"Yes," I say simply.

And I lean up and press my lips to his, pulling his face down to meet mine. I wrap my arms around his neck and I feel like I don't ever want to let go. And at that realization, I pull away, breathless.

"There is a reason. It's because I don't ever want you to leave," I tell him. "I want you to stay here with me. I think I'm falling in love with you."

Quinn sucks in his breath and pulls me back to him. His lips crush mine and he lifts me up. I circle his strong waist with my legs and he holds me there, for what seems like an eternity. I am surrounded by his musky male scent and his muscular arms. I love being in his arms. So I tell him that. And he squeezes me tighter.

I kiss him until I can't breathe.

And then I tell him that I can't breathe.

He laughs and slides me to the ground.

"What am I going to do with you?" he shakes his head. I grin.

"You're going to figure out how to get out of this mess and stay here with me for the rest of the year. And we're going to date. And then you're going to fall in love with me, too."

I stare at him.

He stares back.

"What makes you think that I haven't already gotten started on that?"

I smile. "Have you?"

He nods slowly. "Mia, I've been falling in love with you for weeks."

It's my turn to suck in my breath. And then I kiss him again.

And again.

And again.

And then one more time for good measure.

"We're going to live happily ever after," I tell him.

Quinn stares at me. "Oh, we will, will we? I thought happily ever after was just a fairy tale thing?"

I sniff. "Shows how much you know. Besides, we live in paradise, Quinn. Obviously, we live in a real life fairy tale."

"Hmm," he answers. "I didn't realize that fairy tales had police stations and handcuffs and black eyes. But I'll take your word for it."

He grabs my hand and we continue walking.

"Quinn, my dad will talk to Stefan. And we'll get this sorted out."

Quinn glances at me. "Thank you, Mia. For believing in me so strongly that you went to bat with your father. I know that was hard for you."

I shrug. "It turned out to be pretty painless. So, don't mention it. Until such time that I need to call in a favor and then I'll mention it."

Quinn laughs. "Hmm. Okay. The next time I have to save your topless ass from paparazzi, you can mention it."

I laugh and feel warm, fluttery feelings.

We walk and chat for quite a while longer. Quinn picks me flowers and I carry them. We stop periodically and kiss. And then kiss more. I love the dimple that he gets when he smiles. And I love his lop-sided grin. And the way he always tastes like mint. I tell him these things and he shakes his head, making me realize that I also love it when he shakes his head. So I tell him that, too.

He says that he thinks that my head injury might have done more damage than we originally thought.

So I smack him on the arm.

Then kiss him so more.

After an hour or so, Dante and Reece come out and find us and we sit and have lemonade on the veranda. Reece watches the way I hang onto Quinn's arm with a knowing smile. But she doesn't say anything. And no one has been able to reach Gavin yet. But we put it out of our minds.

It has to work out.

It has to.

Reece and I go change our clothes into sundresses. Mine is hot pink, my new signature color. I wear strappy sandals and pink lip gloss. I've decided that I enjoy being a girly girl. Sort of.

I also blame this on my brain injury.

Dante and Reece have to leave for the christening early, so Quinn and I ride together in Darius' truck. I slide over and sit in the middle.

Our ride is silent, but he reaches over and grabs my hand, holding it on his leg. It feels so good to be here with him. I lay my head on his shoulder and close my eyes.

We have to fix this.

We so have to fix this.

When we arrive at the pier, there is a small crowd already formed. The crowd quickly gets bigger. The Caberrans see this christening as a sign of re-birth. After the assassination attempt last year and the earthquake, it is a step forward. A symbol. It says, *We can move on no matter what obstacles we face.* It causes a lump to form in my throat.

We are allowed to board the boat because we have a personal invitation from Dimitri. So, we stand behind him with Dante and Reece as Dimitri speaks.

He speaks of hope and grace, of strength and patriotism. He speaks of enthusiasm and hard work and faith and love. My throat constricts more with each word that he speaks. Quinn squeezes my hand. I lean into his side.

Finally, the champagne bottle is broken on the side of the beautiful new yacht and the ceremony is over.

Quinn and I take a tour of *The Sunflower* and I am astounded at the beauty of it. It's gorgeous and bright and modern. There are bedrooms and a galley and sitting rooms. There is a wrap-around balcony with a railing and there are reading nooks. There is a hot tub, even. It's a gorgeous boat. But the one thing we don't find on our tour, is Gavin.

Or Stefan.

And that makes me feel nauseas.

How can I plead Quinn's case if I can't find them?

I console myself with crab cakes and a glass of champagne. Quinn has a glass too and reminds me that the drinking age in America is twenty-one. He can't get over that it is legal here for us.

I am not as enthralled with that because this is normal for me.

We make our way to a sitting area on the stern of *The Sunflower*. Surprisingly, there is no one out here and we are alone. I perch on the cushioned edge of the seat and stare out at the rippling turquoise water.

Quinn pulls me into his lap. And he nuzzles my neck and kisses me until I'm breathless. Goosebumps form wherever his lips touch and I shiver from the sheer pleasure of it.

"You're so strong," I tell him as I run my fingers lightly across his chest.

He smiles. "And you're so small."

I smile. "True."

"I feel like you might fit in my pocket," he says conversationally. He pulls me more tightly against him. "Mia, even if I have to go home, we can make it work. Look at Dante and Reece. They managed it, until Dante went to America."

I sigh.

"But they were miserable," I tell him. "That's *why* Dante went to America. And they've been together ever since."

"I know," he says quietly. "But we'll figure it out. Look how much we've overcome already. You had a brain injury for god's sake. And here we are now- you're sitting on my lap and you're in love with me."

"I'm *falling* in love with you," I remind him laughingly. "Don't get ahead of yourself, Awesome One."

He laughs. "Heaven forbid," he answers. "Let me know when you're there, okay? That might be a good thing for me to know."

I laugh, but before I can answer, before I can tell that I do, in fact, love him right now, Reece pops her head out.

"There you are!" She walks out onto the deck. "I've been hunting for you everywhere. Gavin's here. He arrived an hour ago. You should go talk to him, Mia. He might listen to you."

I'm already up and on my way.

Quinn stays with Reece, because that's the smart thing to do. But I weave through the crowded rooms. And I don't see him.

I walk all around the yacht on the deck and don't see him.

I search through the galleys and the reading nooks.

I don't see him.

And then I head to the upper deck.

After walking around the deck walkway, I head down a middle hall. And I hear him laugh. There is no one up here because this is where the bedrooms are.

But I hear him laugh again.

He's definitely here.

I follow the sound.

Right to a bedroom door.

What the hell?

I push the door open and am shocked beyond belief.

It's Gavin alright. And he's naked. And he's not alone.

Gavin and Elena are in bed.

Together.

What.

The.

Hell.

"Mia!" Gavin exclaims. He yanks the bedcovers up over Elena's naked body and I am frozen in the doorway. I can't believe my eyes. A week ago, I would have been devastated because I thought I was falling in love with Gavin.

Thank god I have my memories back and know otherwise.

Because this would have crushed my heart.

"What's going on?" I murmur. I can't tear my eyes away from Gavin's. His are troubled. He didn't want me to see this. That much is apparent.

"What's it look like, Mia? God!" Elena snaps.

And we're clearly back to normal now. Ice Bitch is back to being bitchy. Only now, I've got the upper-hand. I realize that in a rush. They won't want anyone to know about this, so they're at a huge disadvantage. I hate to play hardball with Gavin but the fate of my happiness hangs in the balance.

"Gavin, seriously! Here? On Dimitri's new boat? What the hell do you think he'd say if he knew?" I snap. Gavin looks a bit dismayed.

As he should.

"He won't find out," Gavin says slowly. "And Dante won't either. *Will he*, Mia?"

He looks at me pointedly.

My heart clenches a little. I do love Gavin, even if it is only like a brother or a best friend. I look at Elena.

"Get dressed and get out. I need to talk to Gavin."

She practically snarls at me, but she does pull her clothes on. She flounces past me in a huff. "I'd better not hear people talking about this, Mia. Or there will be hell to pay!"

I don't even bother to answer her. I wait until she's gone and then I close the door. And then I sit next to Gavin.

"Gav, seriously. What are you doing?"

He sighs.

"I don't know. I don't know what I'm doing, apparently. She was rubbing herself on me like she always does and I felt rejected by you and it seemed like a good idea at the time. Obviously, it wasn't. Please tell me you aren't going to tell anyone, Mi."

I reach up and touch his face. His eye is still swollen and black from where Quinn punched him.

"I'm sorry all of this happened," I tell him softly. "I'm sorry that you and Quinn fought. I'm sorry that I drove you to that. I'm sorry that I didn't know what I wanted- and that I led you on, I guess. I didn't mean to, but I did. And I hate that I hurt you, Gav. I love you like a brother- like a best friend. Because you *are* my best friend, and I'm so worried that I've lost you."

I'm crying now. All of a sudden. The tears just start streaking down my face and I wipe at them.

Gavin pulls me to him. He smells like sex, but I ignore that part. I focus instead on the comforting way that he's patting my back.

"Mia, don't cry," he whispers into my hair. "I love you too. And you know what? It's okay. You and I weren't meant to be. We weren't. If we were, we would have realized it a long time ago. You're my best friend, too. And I'm sorry about everything."

I pull away and look at him.

"So, we're good?"

He nods.

"We'll always be good."

I exhale slowly. Knowing that I haven't lost him is the biggest sense of relief I've ever felt. But then I remember why I'm here.

I stare into his eyes.

"Gav, you've got to talk to your dad. It's not right that he's pressing charges against Quinn. Quinn was only protecting himself and you know it."

Gavin looks uncomfortable and fidgets a bit.

"I can't control my dad," he finally says. "You know that. You know how he is."

I nod.

"I do. But in this instance, you've got to. It's not fair to send Quinn back to America now. Not for something that wasn't his fault. You were mad at me, at the situation and you took it out on Quinn. He shouldn't have to pay the price for that."

Gavin is still hesitating, so I have to use my leverage. The leverage that I don't want to use.

"Gav, if you make your father drop the charges, I will never breathe a word of what I saw here today. Ever. Not to anyone. Not to Reece, not to Dante, not to Dante's father."

Gavin stares at me, his gaze a bit cool.

"And if I don't?"

I shrug. "Let's not worry about that, okay? Because I know you'll do the right thing and make your father drop this."

The moment is charged. Gavin's eyes are pissed. I can see that. But he has to know that I'm right. And the fact that I even had to use this situation as leverage make me angry too.

"Gavin, this is ridiculous. You're a better person than this. You know what the right thing to do is. You're a good person—just do the right thing."

We're having a stare-down. His dark gaze meets mine. And holds.

And holds.

And holds until I grow fidgety and uncomfortable.

And then finally he sighs.

"Fine. You're right. I was pissed because things didn't turn out the way I'd hoped. I'll talk to my father tonight. We'll get it straightened out. You're right. Quinn doesn't deserve this."

A rush of relief floods through me.

"Thank you," I murmur. I reach over and grab his hand. "Thank you. I appreciate this so much."

He nods. "I know. And it's the right thing to do. I'm sorry that he was arrested in the first place. My dad was angry and I couldn't talk him out of it."

"I know," I tell him. "That's exactly what we thought happened."

Gavin gets dressed and we find Dante, Reece and Quinn. Before anyone can say anything, Gavin steps forward and holds his hand out to Quinn.

Quinn shakes it without hesitation.

"I'm sorry," Gavin tells him. "I shouldn't have punched you. Or shoved you. It wasn't your fault that the situation frustrated me. I hope you can forgive me. I'm going to talk to my dad tonight and convince him to drop the charges."

Quinn nods and accepts his apology. And then we all sit and chat for another hour. It's so surreal that I can't even believe that it's happening.

But it is.

And we actually have fun, all curled up on the stern of *The Sunflower*, sipping at champagne and eating appetizers. We laugh, we joke, and things almost seem normal. I don't say a word about finding Gavin with Elena and I don't see her again all evening. Gavin doesn't even seem to notice her absence.

Later in the night, after we go back to Giliberti House, Gavin calls and tells me that his father agreed to let the whole thing go.

I exhale a long sigh of relief and I feel like the weight of the world has slipped from my shoulders. I didn't even realize how uptight I was about it until this moment. And in this moment, I feel like I could fly.

So I fly down the hall and tell Quinn the good news.

It is morning before I creep quietly back to my own room.

Apparently, New Mia's boyfriend is sexy as hell and has mad-bedroom-skills.

I smile as I close my bedroom door softly behind me. My knees are still weak, but I don't meow at myself this time. Anyone's knees would be weak after the night that I had.

Chapter Twenty - Three

Two Months Later

Reece and I are meowing at Quinn.

This is not unusual. Every chance we get, we do it. It's hilarious. Or we're just easily entertained. One or the other.

This time, it is because Quinn is refusing to wear a speedo in the normal European fashion. He insists on sticking to swim trunks. Although the point of him wearing a suit at all is sort of moot. He still can't swim.

We're at the beach today. Dante and Reece stayed in Caberra and school finally resumed after construction was complete, but we're out for Christmas break now. It's been a hectic and stressful past couple of months.

We've worked our tails off, volunteering on different clean-up committees, to get Valese back to the beautiful, pristine city that it should be. And we've succeeded. You almost can't tell that an earthquake ever hit.

Sadly, the construction on my own home is almost finished and I'll be moving back home within the month. I say sadly because I love being out at Giliberti House with Quinn, Dante and Reece. But I'll just have to make the drive to visit them after I move.

Every day.

Maybe even twice a day.

"Quinn, just grow a pair and wear the speedo," Gavin shouts from down the beach.

He and Quinn have patched up their differences in the way that only boys can and even consider each other a friend again. It will never cease to amaze me how boys can get mad, get in a physical fight and then get over it. The male species is truly weird.

Gavin shouts again, louder this time for effect. "Just grow a set!"

Quinn runs him down, then tackles him to the ground and they roll in the sand for a bit. Somehow, and I don't exactly know how, Gavin's speedos end up floating on the waves of the sea.

Reece and I look at each other and laugh before we resume looking at our magazines from the safety of our beach chairs. The boys rough-house for a while longer and then Dante joins them to throw a Frisbee around.

As I look around, at my laughing friends, at the beautiful sea, at my BFF next to me, I can't believe how lucky I am. Life really does seem like a fairy tale.

But even fairy tales come to an end. I swallow hard as I remember that sad fact. We're all looking at colleges now and I know that our happy little group will split apart next year. Gavin and I are looking at Cambridge, while Dante and Reece are looking at colleges in the States. Quinn hasn't decided yet what he'd like to do. I'm hoping that he will come with me, though.

Yes, that is selfish.

But honestly, Cambridge? It's not exactly like it's a hardship.

And even though some things end, endings are just doors closing so that new doors can open, right?

I watch Quinn now, his muscles flexing and moving as he dives to catch the Frisbee. He holds it up, showing the others that he did, in fact, catch it before it hit the ground. Then he crows because he won.

He makes his way over to me and with the sunlight shining from behind him, he is heart-stoppingly gorgeous.

Seriously.

I squint up at him as he holds a hand out.

"Yes?" I ask him, then grin.

"Come on," he tells me. "You've got a deal to uphold."

I'm confused and I tell him that. He smiles.

"You were supposed to teach me to swim months ago. And you haven't yet."

I consider that.

"True," I tell him. "But we've been busy with other things. Like, you know, rebuilding a city."

He laughs and pulls me to my feet.

"Excuses, excuses," he chuckles. "I don't see a hammer in your hand right now. I think you can fit me in."

He wraps his arm around my waist and I tuck myself into his side. We walk leisurely down the beach and I stare up at him.

"I'm lucky," I tell him suddenly. And he looks down at me in surprise.

"Why is that?"

"Because I've got my very own American Cowboy."

He smiles and shakes his head. "I've told you. You don't have to keep calling me that. Awesome One will do."

I roll my eyes.

But he *is* awesome. I'm just never going to admit that to him. He's cocky enough as it is... but that's just the way I like him.

The sun beats down on our shoulders as we walk down to a pier. The sea laps softly at the wood and I stare down at the clear water.

I tell him again the mechanics of swimming.

And he nods.

"Got it," he tells me. "Keep my head up, relax and float. I can do it."

I nod. "Yes, you can. And I'll be right there with you."

He laughs. "I think we've established this, Mi. You can't save me. You're half my size."

I roll my eyes.

"I've saved you already," I tell him. "I've saved you from an empty life without me in it."

I'm totally joking, of course, but he nods. He seems thoughtful.

"Mia," he says huskily, as he pulls me to him. "I was just wondering about something. Remember a couple of months ago…you said you were falling for me. Then you said you weren't quite there. You were going to let me know when you were, but you've never said anything."

He pauses.

And pauses.

And looks at me with an eyebrow raised.

I sigh happily. And smile.

"I'm there," I tell him. "I love you, Quinn McKeyen. I thought you already knew."

He grins and my knees weaken.

"I do," he admits. "I've known all along. I just wanted to hear you say it."

"I love you," I tell him softly. Then I lean up on my tiptoes and whisper into his ear. "I love you. Forever and ever and ever."

He grins and grabs my hand.

"Forever and ever and ever?" He raises an eyebrow now.

I nod. "Yep. I told you—this is our own personal fairy tale."

He laughs and I squeeze his hand.

"On three, okay?"

He nods.

We count to three.

And then we jump.

About the Author

Courtney Cole is a novelist who lives near Lake Michigan with her pet iPad, her domestic zoo (aka family) and her favorite cashmere socks. She is always working on her next project.

To learn more about her, visit
www.courtneycolewrites.com